JOHN RUSSELL FEARN'S
THE GOLDEN AMAZON

SEETEE SUN

JOHN RUSSELL FEARN'S
THE GOLDEN AMAZON

SEETEE SUN

JOHN GLASBY

The Golden Amazon, Book 22

WILDSIDE PRESS

INTRODUCTION

AND SO…THE GOLDEN AMAZON SAGA CONTINUES!

IT gives me great pleasure to introduce this new Golden Amazon novel, the 22nd title in Wildside's reboot of one of the most amazing series of science fiction novels ever published. Amazing because the Golden Amazon was originally created by John Russell Fearn way back in 1944, and was intended as a one-off book! Fortunately the novel was reprinted by the Toronto *Star Weekly* in 1945, and massive reader approbation led to the initially villainous Amazon being resurrected as a super-heroine, and returning in numerous sequels in the *Star Weekly*.

The long running series finally came to an end with the premature death of its creator in 1960. With the approval of the author's widow, the Scott Meredith Literary Agency then tried to find other writers to continue the series for the Toronto *Star Weekly*. But none of the authors they tried could duplicate Fearn's unique "popular" style, handicapped as they were by not being provided with a sufficiently detailed dossier on the character.

The *Star Weekly* Amazon series ran to 24 titles. During Fearn's lifetime, only the first six had been reprinted in book form. The first complete reprinting in book form was accomplished by Gary Lovisi's small press Gryphon Books between 1996 and 2009, and added two further posthumous titles, making 26 in total.

The Amazon series fell into two phases. The first six books were set in the near future and the action was limited to Earth, Venus and Mars. Following book # 7, moving further into the future, the scope expanded to include the outer planets, then Alpha Centauri, before moving far out into interstellar space—and beyond!

Fearn's final novel, *Earth Divided* had ended on a cliffhanger, which Fearn had intended to resolve in his next novel. But with the failure of other writers to take up the baton, it looked very much as if the Golden Amazon had ran her last race. But, using Fearn's own fragmentary notes written just before he died, and utilizing the plots of two of his non-Amazon short stories, I myself wrote a new 27th novel, *Chameleon Planet* which Gryphon printed in 2006.

Following its first publication I had then invited other writers—clients of my Cosmos Literary agency—to accept the challenge of continuing the saga. I avoided the earlier error of the *Star Weekly* by providing writers with a sample novel and a detailed dossier. Of the authors who expressed interest, the first to step forward and actually deliver a complete new novel was John Glasby.

The good news for all fans of the Amazon is that John made a superb fist of it with his first attempt! *Seetee Sun* was written with all of Fearn's trademark fast-action verve and imagination, but also contained all the strengths of Glasby's own style, honed over a long literary career.

If any author was born to continue the Golden Amazon, that man was John Glasby, whose career uncannily paralleled Fearn's own. Glasby completed a further three Amazon novels before his own death in 2010. All four were published in very limited small press editions by Gryphon Books, and have been long out of print.

Beginning in 2012, all of Fearn's "later phase" (from # 7 to 27) Amazon novels have been issued sequentially in paperback by Wildside, renumbered as 1 through 21, and they remain in print. And now, Wildside will be issuing the remaining four Glasby Amazons, beginning with *Seetee Sun* (book # 22 in the rebooted series.)

John Stephen Glasby was born in 1928, and graduated from Nottingham University with an honours degree in Chemistry. He started his career as a research chemist for I.C.I. in 1952, and worked for them until his retirement. Over the next two decades, be began a parallel career as a an extraordinarily prolific writer of science fiction novels and short stories, his first novels appearing in the summer of 1952 from Curtis Warren Ltd, under various house pseudonyms such as "Rand Le Page" and "Berl Cameron," as was the fashion of the day. Late in 1952, he began an astonishing association with the London publisher John Spencer Ltd., which was to last more than twenty years.

Thus was forged the first of many parallels with John Russell Fearn, who in 1950 had become involved with another similar London publisher, Scion Ltd. Like Fearn, Glasby quickly became their mainstay author, writing hundreds of stories and novels to their commissions in several genres. Eventually these commissions embraced an even wider number of fields than Fearn had worked in. Not only was Glasby required to switch back and forth from science fiction to supernatural stories (his preferred mediums), but also foreign legion, Second World War novels, hospital romances, crime novels, and westerns. Like Fearn, he amassed a large number of personal pseudonyms, the best known being "A. J. Merak," under which name a number of his science fiction novels were reprinted in the 1960s in the U.S.A.

When his association with John Spencer eventually ended, he took the opportunity to sell a science fiction novel under his own name to Don Wollheim at Ace Books (*Project Jove*, 1971). Always a great fan of the work of H. P. Lovecraft, he then wrote a collection of Mythos stories for August Derlerth at Arkham House. Derlerth suggested extensive revisions and improvements, which Glasby duly followed, but Derlerth unfortunately died before it could be published, and the book was returned.

Always interested in astronomy since childhood, he had joined the variable star section of the British Astronomical Society in 1958, and was made Director in 1965. He was elected a Fellow of the Royal astronomical Society in 1960, and he has published numerous textbooks and encyclopaedias on astronomy and chemistry, the first being *Variable Stars* in 1968.

In later years, following his retirement, Glasby returned to writing more supernatural stories and novels in the Lovecraftian vein, culminating in an ambitious trilogy, *Dark Armageddon* that unified and brought to a climatic conclusion Lovecraft's Cthulhu Mythos cycle (posthumously published by Lume Books in 2017.)

During the 1960s, Glasby prolifically wrote western paperbacks, just as Fearn had done in the previous decade. All of these dozens of westerns were reprinted many years later, and their success prompted Glasby to write new westerns, along with science fiction and mysteries, until his death in 2010.

Glasby also became a regular contributor to my science fiction and supernatural anthology series, *Fantasy Adventures* (Wildside Press) with both sf and supernatural stories.

Glasby was the ideal choice of author to continue the Golden Amazon series, because, like Fearn, he had a treasure-chest of previously published material to draw upon for inspiration. In *Seetee Sun*, buffs of British science fiction may detect some resonances with Glasby's 1950s series of interstellar adventure stories featuring the crew of the space ship *Astra II*. However, *Seetee Sun* is essentially a brand new work, taking the Cosmic Crusaders forward—not backward.

Watch out for the remaining new John Glasby adventures of the Golden Amazon from Wildside Press: they are not to be missed!

—Philip Harbottle
May, 2023.

CHAPTER I

SLAVERS FROM SPACE

STANDING before the huge visiplate in the vast control room of the Ultra, Abna of Atlantis scrutinized the view spread across the whole of the ship's forward scanning system. A Greek God of a man, standing seven feet tall, he was the first to have been revived from the drug-induced sleep while the ship had been in hyperspace. Before leaving normal space their course had been plotted into the ship's computer so as to approach the outermost environs of the galaxy, to the furthermost point in the Milky Way system—and this showed quite clearly on the view in front of him.

The Ultra was now moving at just below light speed slowing gradually as he manipulated the controls with swift, sure movements. Towards the right-hand side of the screen, the stars of the galactic arm glittered brilliantly in their thousands but in the other direction there was only blackness with just a handful of lonely, isolated suns scattered across it. Out there lay the empty intergalactic gulf which separated the galaxy from the multitude of others, a few of which were visible only as faint wisps of bright nebulosity billions of light years away.

The sound of the mighty atomic engines was little more than a muted whisper now they had dropped out of hyperspace. Just before going into hyperdrive, a check had shown that the fuel needed for the atomic engines was running dangerously low. But their luck had held. They had found an uninhabited world orbiting a dying red star where they had located a supply of copper, the chemical element upon which the engines relied for the nuclear reactions going on deep within the vessel.

As he glanced down at the velocimeter there was a faint movement behind him and Abna's wife, the black-clad Golden Amazon, a magnificently perfect figure of a woman, came forward to stand at his elbow. "Where exactly are we now?" she asked, her beautiful violet eyes taking in every small detail of the view.

"At the moment we seem to be still on course moving along the very rim of the galaxy," Abna replied without taking his glance off the visiscreen. He pointed to a faint gleaming oval of light. "Over there is the Andromeda Nebula." Reaching down, he slowly turned one of the dials on the large control board.

The oval expanded swiftly as the telescope midway along the sleek length of the Ultra magnified the image a thousand times, resolving the nebula into a vast agglomeration of stars. A little way below it on the screen, a smaller patch of misty light was visible. Satisfied, he added. "And that is over two million light years away."

"Are you sure that is Andromeda out there?" the Amazon asked.

"Quite sure. That smaller cluster is a companion nebula, rather like the Greater and Lesser Magellanic Clouds which are satellites of our galaxy."

Before he could say anything more, the remaining three superhuman members of the Cosmic Crusaders entered the control room. Viona, the vibrant and youthful copper-haired daughter of Abna and the Amazon, and Viona's husband Mexone, tall and broad-shouldered, came to stand a little way behind them. They made up the original quartet of the Crusaders but since their adventures on the planet Karg they had been joined by Thania, a teenager who had undergone the necessary surgery to change her into one of them, possessing all of their superhuman powers.

Thania was the first of the three to speak, still finding it difficult to comprehend all of the wonders of space travel. "Is that where you're thinking of going?" she asked, a trifle breathlessly.

The Golden Amazon shook her head. "Even if we were to travel faster than light, it would still take us a considerable time to reach Andromeda. Somehow, I think there are more—" She broke off abruptly.

Without warning, the Ultra came to a shuddering stop. The muted hum of the engines could still be heard indicating there was no fault with them. Bracing herself against the controls, she managed to remain on her feet. Even so, she had to exert all of the superhuman strength in her arms to prevent herself crashing into the metal panels.

Abna too was still upright but the other three had not been so lucky. All of them had been thrown heavily to the metal floor.

Swiftly, the Amazon and Abna lifted them from where they had fallen. Fortunately, none of them seemed to have suffered much physical hurt with only Mexone nursing his right arm where he had been slammed hard against the wall.

Around them, the exterior plates of the Ultra now shrieked and groaned as if some terrific pressure was being applied to them.

The Amazon grasped the situation at once. "Cut the engines! Quickly!" she ordered. "Whatever that is out there, the hull will collapse if the engines keep thrusting us forward against it."

Without waiting to ask any questions, Viona ran to the side of the console and pulled down the switch. A deafening silence shrouded the ship as the powerful engines stopped.

Pulling in a deep breath, the Amazon muttered harshly through her teeth: "Now let's see what we've got here. This is something I've never experienced before."

Peering into the visiscreen, Mexone said evenly, "I can see nothing in front of us." His tone radiated puzzlement. "There's certainly nothing visible, anyway. My guess would be that there is some force out there preventing us from continuing on this course."

"You mean something produced by a highly advanced civilization?" It was the first thing to come into the Amazon's mind.

Mexone nodded. "I can't think of anything else. We know there are powerful magnetic fields in various parts of the galaxy, possibly strong enough to stop us in our tracks like this. But if this is one of them I would have expected it to affect the instruments in some way." His keen gaze took in the entire length of the controls. As far as he could see everything was functioning normally.

The Amazon glanced obliquely at her husband. "Where would you estimate the nearest inhabited planetary system is? You were the first to be revived. Did you notice any in this vicinity?"

Shaking his head, Abna depressed a switch. After a few moments, he said, "See for yourself, Vi. The scanner gives no indication of intelligent life within forty light years. You have to remember that this is a sparsely populated region of the galaxy. I wouldn't expect to find much sign of life here."

"Then we have a problem," the Amazon replied gravely. "Either this is a natural phenomenon, one we've never come across before— or there is a highly advanced civilization here and they clearly have no intention of allowing any intruders into their region of space."

Turning her head slowly, she glanced at each of the others in turn. "Anyone got any ideas?"

There was a long silence. Then, with a glance towards the star-strewn blackness in front of the Ultra, Viona said, "Whatever it is, it's evidently strong enough to stop the ship even when it was traveling at well over half light velocity—yet it allows light to pass through it. My guess would be that it's a force field of some kind."

The Amazon ran her fingers through her long blonde hair. During their travels through the galaxy they had encountered many strange phenomena but this was something they had never met before—a totally invisible barrier closing off an entire region of space.

The same notion had also occurred to Abna. Turning away from the controls, he said quietly, choosing his words with care, "I suggest that the first thing we should do is try to determine its extent and then use a missile to see just how strong it really is."

"If it can stop the Ultra dead in its tracks, I don't see that a missile will do anything," Mexone argued.

The Amazon's lips curved into a faint smile. "Assuming we can reverse to a safe distance, it's just possible a nuclear bomb might have some effect." Her expression hardened into grim lines of determination. "If there is an intelligent life form behind this, I want to know what—and where—it is. Any race sufficiently advanced to produce a spatial barrier like this could be a threat to this entire region of the galaxy if they should have warlike intentions."

"I agree." Abna ran a finger down his cheek, deep in thought. "If they can cut off a whole region of space in this way, I shudder to think what they could do if they declared war on anyone."

Stepping up to the console, knowing that everything would have to be performed quickly and correctly if the Ultra was not to be damaged by any further pressure against the barrier, the Amazon's fingers moved deftly over the controls. At a signal from her, Viona pushed up the lever to restart the atomic engines. Immediately, the Amazon threw the vessel into reverse; powerful forward rockets firing within seconds.

Slowly, the Ultra backed away from the obstruction that barred its path. Letting her pent-up breath go in small pinches through her teeth, she slowly turned the vessel, taking the Ultra back half a million miles before swinging it round again onto its original course.

In front of them there was nothing to indicate the presence of anything out of the ordinary. As far as they could determine the stars all around them, in every conceivable direction, shone with their normal luster. There was nothing to suggest that ahead of them, only a short distance away on the galactic scale, something existed; something as yet beyond their comprehension.

Each of them was engrossed in endless speculations. Did this barrier extend all the way across this section of the galaxy? Was it a purely local formation, like a huge bubble, effectively sealing off a comparatively small number of planetary systems in this region?

Had it been produced by some singular physical alignment of suns and planets, their individual magnetic fields intermeshing in some unique manner—or was there some super race scientifically capable of erecting such a vast and potent obstacle as this? If so, what was the motive behind it?

The Amazon's voice broke in on their thoughts. "Now we have a choice. Either we use the Ultra again and approach that shield along a different course, and from a different direction—or do we split up and take two of our small safety machines and approach it from two widely separated points? We keep them as emergency lifeboats, but we can just as well use them for local exploratory work."

"The latter method would undoubtedly save time," Abna suggested, "and the pinnaces can be maneuvered more easily."

"Very well." Nodding in acquiescence, the Amazon continued, "I'll remain on board the Ultra. Abna and Viona will take one of the small vessels and Mexone and Thania will take the other. We'll keep in touch with the ultraradio."

This was a device the Amazon had perfected. It converted words into both radio and light that was then transformed back into speech by the receiver. It had the advantage of overcoming interstellar static.

Ten minutes later, the two pinnaces were ready. Standing in front of the controls, the Amazon opened the airlock and watched them depart; two tiny vessels in comparison with the Ultra, their atomic exhausts showing as thin pencils of light against the eternal dark of space, dwindling rapidly into the distance.

* * * *

In the tiny craft, Abna reduced their velocity while they were still an estimated quarter of a million miles from where he judged the barrier to be. There was no point in taking unnecessary risks. These craft did not possess the strength of the Ultra and in the forefront of his mind he could visualize what would happen if they struck this shield with any real velocity.

Beside him, Viona sat peering intently through the small screen. She could see nothing out of the ordinary. A blue-white sun glared at her from a distance of several light years and there was a smaller, red star, which she judged was somewhat closer. In front of them, the ultraradio suddenly broke into sound.

"Have you reached it yet, Viona?"

Flicking down the switch, she said tautly, "There's nothing yet, Mother. We've cut our velocity and so far everything seems to be normal."

"Then be careful. I don't want to scrape the pinnaces off that shield—or whatever it is."

The impact came within seconds and almost broke the broad straps holding her in her seat. Tensing the muscles in her arms, she grabbed the edge of the chair and kept herself from hurtling forward. Beside her, Abna said loudly so that the Amazon could pick up his voice, "We've just come up against it. From our present spatial co-ordinates I'd say this barrier, or whatever it is, could be several light years in extent. There doesn't appear to be any way through it."

He picked up the faint sound as the Amazon whistled through her teeth. "Mexone and Thania have just reported. Their result is the same as yours. If we assume the barrier is likely to be in the shape of a vast sphere, it's quite clear now that we're dealing with something on a truly interstellar scale. You'd all better return to the Ultra. Somehow, we have to get to the bottom of this."

Half an hour later they were all assembled in the control room. With the atomic engines off and the vessel motionless in space, there was no sound throughout the whole length of the ship. While they had been away, the Amazon had brought out several star maps and these were spread out on the large table.

Abna eyed them with an expression of surprise on his handsome features. "I thought you intended to see what the effect of a nuclear bomb might be," he said.

"Oh, I still intend doing that," the Amazon said crisply. "But first I think we should discover the locations of all possible planetary systems in this region of the galaxy, say within two hundred light years of our present position. Firstly, I don't want to destroy any civilizations nearby in the event that a nuclear bomb might start a chain reaction in whatever it is out there."

"And secondly?" Viona prompted as her mother paused.

The Amazon straightened. "I also want to know if there are any planetary systems in this neighborhood which might show peculiar characteristics."

"What kind of peculiar characteristics?" Thania inquired, a look of puzzlement on her youthful face.

"Anything we've never come across before which might explain what we have here. As far as I'm aware this is unique in the galaxy."

"And even if we find something which might possibly explain it, what good will it be if even a nuclear bomb fails to pierce that barrier?"

"We'll cross that bridge when we come to it," the Amazon replied with a slight hint of reproval in her voice.

The Amazon soon found the star chart she wanted and placed it on top of the others, studying it closely. At first sight she could see nothing that caught her attention. Being a sparsely populated region there were perhaps forty stars marked on it. All seemed to be quite normal stars and it was possible that many of them had planetary systems orbiting around them. There was nothing to pick out one from the others as being abnormal in any way.

Sighing in exasperation, she made to move away; then stopped as Mexone said, "What about this one? It's the only one different from the rest." His finger pointed to an object very close to the galactic rim.

Bending forward, the Amazon studied it carefully, her lips pressed into a tight line. Now that she studied it in detail she saw what Mexone had noticed. The photographic image appeared fuzzy, unlike the other star-like points. Moistening her lips she said tautly, "I think we should examine this with the telescope. It may be nothing more than a fault on the photograph."

Once at the controls, the Amazon manipulated the onboard telescope with deft movements of her fingers, aligning the instrument on the star in question. Swiftly, she brought it into the center of the viewing screen. One look was sufficient to tell them why its appearance on the star chart had appeared strange.

It was a double star, each component revolving around their common center of gravity. The larger of the two was a brilliant blue giant star, the smaller one being yellow and cooler, apparently not too dissimilar to Sol. During their voyaging through the galaxy the Cosmic Crusaders had seen many similar double-star systems. So what could be different about this one?

"Can we get any more magnification from the telescope?" she asked suddenly, not looking up.

Abna immediately guessed what was in her mind. "You want to know if there are any planets in that system? I'd say both things are highly unlikely. My guess is that particular double star is at least seventy light years away. It would be stretching the telescope to its limits and so far, we've never found a double star system with the two components as close together as that with any planets. Their interacting gravitational fields would make planetary formation virtually impossible. What makes you think this could be an exception?"

"Let's just call it a hunch. I've got a feeling something out there is responsible for what we've found and so far, that's the only likely candidate." The Amazon turned the dial up to its maximum position.

On the screen, the image expanded swiftly. Watching it, she had the feeling they were swooping towards it, being drawn irresistibly through the blackness towards those two glittering points of light. Around the edges of the visiscreen, the others stars drifted off the sides until only the two stars remained in the center.

Using the highest magnification possible, they were just able to discern the three tiny specks of light. Two of them were bright crescents some distance from the suns and clearly they revolved in orbits around both. The third, however, was just visible between the blue and yellow stars.

Abna pursed his lips. "That is distinctly odd," he said after a momentary pause. "Either that planet only revolves around one of the suns or it forms a figure of eight orbit about both. This might be the answer. The only problem remaining is how to reach it."

Less than half an hour later, they fired a hydrogen bomb at the barrier from a safe distance. Tensely, they waited until the missile struck. Even from a distance of hundreds of miles, the explosion was clearly visible, a vivid flash of nuclear violence. The vicious glare diminished slowly.

The Amazon shook her blonde head in apparent bewilderment. Finally, she said, "It would seem that not even a hydrogen bomb can cause any damage to that screen." A frown creased her forehead as she went on, "And it would take us weeks, possibly months, to determine its full extent and whether there is any way through it."

Abna smiled faintly. "It would seem that, for the first time, we've come up against something out of our reach."

"You're not just going to turn around and leave it at this, are you?" Viona exclaimed. "I thought the purpose of the Crusaders was to examine anything which might prove a threat to the galaxy."

"It is," her mother retorted. "But what do you suggest we do? We can't break through that barrier. For some reason, all of those suns in that region of space are enclosed within an impenetrable shield and at the moment, I can think of nothing we have aboard the Ultra which will allow us to get inside."

There was a long moment of silence, than Abna ran a hand down his cheek, a thoughtful expression on his face. "There might be a way," he said finally. "Maybe we can't get through it in normal space-time but if that shield out there exists only in space and time, we might succeed in hyperspace."

The Amazon reflected on that for a moment; then nodded. "It might work," she agreed. "But it could be dangerous. If you're wrong and we hit it at hyperspeed it would almost certainly mean the end of the Ultra—and of us." Her words fell into a chilling silence.

At the back of her mind was the thought that if whoever had put up this interstellar shield was sufficiently advanced to perform such a colossal feat of scientific achievement, they might also have considered the possibility of other races having the hyperdrive and had taken the necessary precautions. A moment later, however, she dismissed the notion.

The Cosmic Crusaders were all dedicated to their work of combating any race that might have warlike tendencies and she was unwilling to shy away from this in spite of the obvious risk. Turning to look at each oft hem in turn, she asked, "Are you all willing to take this chance?"

There was no hesitation from any of them. They all nodded in reply to her question.

"Very well, we'll do it." She turned to Abna. "Plot a course for that double star and then prepare to go into hyperdrive." To Thania she said, "This is going to be uncomfortable for a little while. We have to accelerate to near light velocity and slip into hyperspace before we reach that screen."

Once Abna had plotted the coordinates of the double star into the Ultra's computer, they stood ready as the Amazon fed as much power into the engines to build up maximum velocity before their entry into hyperspace. The faster their initial velocity, the shorter would be their duration in hyperspace. Although their velocity would be many times faster than light, relative to the normal universe, no further acceleration was possible once they were in hyperspace.

The Ultra leapt forward like a maddened beast. Acceleration clawed at them, pushing them back into their seats. The Amazon and Abna joined the others in their reclining seats. The tremendous strain increased until it reached a point where it seemed they could stand it no longer. Muscles bulged under their tights as the pull on their bodies increased.

The Crusaders allowed themselves to drift into unconsciousness. Injections from tiny instruments in their seats put them into a deeper sleep akin to suspended animation.

In normal space-time it was impossible for any object to attain light speed, so the Ultra became encased in a field of force that increased to a level where it could no longer be contained in the normal universe, so that it slipped out of normal space into another dimension where it *could* exist—hyperspace. Here, space was foreshortened and the distance traveled was equivalent to the ship having traveled many times faster than light. This discovery, more than anything else, had opened up the entire galaxy for space exploration.

The Ultra's computer calculated the distance traveled in hyperspace, and when the 70 light years had been covered, reviving injections restored the Crusaders to consciousness.

Inside the Ultra the strain suddenly ceased. Now there was no gravity. The spaceship seemed to be hanging in a void in which nothing except the Ultra existed. Floating aimlessly inside the huge cabin, they tried to orientate themselves. Then Abna pulled himself along the control panel and threw the switch that returned normal gravity. Dropping to the floor, their leg muscles cushioned the impact.

On a galactic scale, the distance they would travel through hyperspace was short. Yet every second, they expected the hull to burst open as they hit that shield and project them into the absolute nothingness which existed all around them. They all held their breath but nothing happened. When the field was collapsed and they eventually dropped out of hyperspace, the Ultra still seemed to be intact and they were alive.

Staring at the visiscreen, the Amazon said briskly, "We've made it. It would seem our plan worked." On the wide screen was a clear view of the dual sun system. A quick mental calculation told the Amazon they had emerged from hyperspace within a hundred million miles of the larger blue star. It blazed brilliantly towards the lower left of the screen, its light blotting out much of the view.

With a swift movement, she stepped up to the screen and reduced the eye-searing glare. The yellow sun now showed an appreciable disc. As they had previously estimated, it was Sol-sized. For the moment, however, she gave the two completely dissimilar stars only a cursory glance, fixing the whole other attention on the planets.

Of the two outer worlds, one was obviously a gas giant resembling Jupiter. The other, somewhat closer to the central suns appeared Earth-like and even from that distance it was possible to see that it was cloud-covered with hints of brown, blue and green just visible on the surface.

"Well, what do you think now that we're here?" Abna asked.

The Amazon continued to stare at the screen without speaking, almost as if she hadn't heard the question. Then she turned slowly and there was a look of mystification in her violet eyes. "We saw three planets in this system, didn't we? Then where is the third, the one we thought might orbit both of those suns?"

They all looked again but as the Amazon had said, there were only two worlds visible. Inexplicably the third, that in which they were most interested, seemed to have vanished!

"It can't have simply disappeared," Mexone muttered. "And we all saw it. Unless it's eclipsed by one of those suns. Or perhaps it was some malfunction of the telescope."

"Somehow, I don't think either of those two explanations is correct." Abna shook his head. "We're too high above the orbital plane of this system for any occultation to be possible and the telescopic image was far too clear."

The Amazon drew in a deep breath as she reached a sudden decision. "I suggest our only course is to land on that Earth-type planet. If there is any life there with a reasonably high intelligence, we may learn something from them. Once we put the Ultra into a stable orbit around that planet, we'll take two of the pinnaces onto the surface."

"You mean you'll leave the Ultra without anyone on board?" There was a note of undisguised astonishment in Thania's voice. "But if there is a warlike race somewhere in this vicinity, won't they—?"

"Attack the Ultra?" the Amazon smiled. "Take my word for it, Thania, the Ultra is perfectly capable of taking care of itself."

Once in orbit around the planet, they spent the best part of an hour taking readings with the various instruments on board. As with any new world, it was necessary to be absolutely certain of the conditions on the surface before venturing down. Finally, they were satisfied. The atmosphere was approximately the same as Earth with just a slightly higher percentage of oxygen. There were several large land masses, and three large oceans. Nowhere, however, was there any sign of an advanced civilization; no cities or towns showed on the ultra-scanners. Much of the land appeared to be covered by dense jungle.

The Amazon strapped on her belt and checked the protonic blaster before returning it to its holster. She waited patiently while the others did likewise, her critical gaze still fixed on the screen. Her initial impression was that this planet was still in the early stages of its evolution and that if rational, thinking creatures did exist here, they had not yet climbed far up the ladder of scientific achievement. It was not what she had hoped for and in spite of its outward appearance there was something here that disturbed her more than she cared to admit, even to herself.

As they made their way along the curving corridor towards the pinnaces, she voiced her doubts to the others. "Do any of you have the feeling that there's something wrong about this world? Maybe I'm over-reacting but I would have expected some sign of fairly advanced technology here. That yellow sun looks about as old as Sol, yet there's nothing to indicate that anything has evolved beyond the beast level."

Viona made an observation. "There's one obvious pointer which might explain it. We haven't taken that other sun into account. My guess is that it's pouring out deadly ultra-violet radiation at a terrific rate. Any humanoid life might never have had a chance to evolve."

From just behind them, Abna said, "Whatever the answer it, perhaps we'll find it once we get down there. It's quite possible they wiped themselves out in a nuclear war some time in the past. Unfortunately we can't test for any radioactivity until we get to the surface."

CHAPTER 2

SYMBIOSIS

DROPPING out of space, the two pinnaces hit the atmosphere at a shallow angle, skipping across it like a flat stone over water, to reduce their velocity. Through the clouds, they made out huge stretches of jungle with wide rivers flowing through them. The odd effect of the double sunlight produced a curious prismatic color on the surface, predominately green but in places it was yellow and in others blue. They deliberately made a double circuit of the planet, examining the night side for any evidence of lights but there was nothing.

"If there is any advanced civilization here, they either live completely underground or they have no need of light," the Amazon observed. "We'll land on the day side near the terminator. If we do that we shouldn't have long to wait for night to see if they are nocturnal folk."

They landed in a wide, open space within a mile of a broad river. The suits they wore were lightweight and flexible having been designed by the Amazon. Climbing down onto the surface she threw a quick glance all around her.

The sky overhead was a pale green, a blend of the blue and yellow radiation from the two suns but already it was changing to a deep blue light for the yellow sun was slowly slipping down towards the horizon.

The other Crusaders came forward to join her, their hands close to their weapons. Abna held the radiation counter in his left hand. Apart from a few clicks, it remained quiescent. "There seems to be scarcely any radioactivity at all." His voice echoed over the small communicators they each had in their helmet.

The Amazon nodded. "The atmosphere also seems to be breathable. I think we can discard the helmets." Taking hers off, she shook her blonde hair until it fell about her shoulders.

There was a slight breeze bringing a host of indefinable odors from the direction of the thick jungle around the periphery of the clearing. Now they had taken off their helmets, sounds also reached them; vague clicking noises, interspersed by curious high-pitched howls.

Before doing anything more, the Amazon took a small spectroscope from her pocket. "I want to get a spectrum of that yellow sun before it vanishes below the horizon," she said in reply to Abna's mute look of inquiry. Sighting the instrument on the sun, she peered through it intently for a moment; then pressed a small button. The printout of the spectrum emerged from the bottom.

"That's strange," she murmured to herself.

"What is it?" Viona came to stand at her mother's shoulder, peering down at the narrow oblong strip.

"This can't be right." Turning swiftly, the Amazon repeated the procedure. The second spectrum was identical with the first. "I've never seen anything like this before. I would have expected the spectrum of that sun to be virtually the same as Sol's but—"

"Let me see." Abna took the two spectra from her and perused them closely in the bluish light. His face assumed a puzzled frown. "It's almost the reverse of what I would have anticipated."

He showed it to the others who all shook their heads in bewilderment. Thania, of course, had never seen the spectrum of Sol and could therefore give no opinion or explanation.

"There's one thing we can be sure of," the Amazon said at length. "That yellow sun out there isn't a white dwarf or even a neutron star which might have explained this. It's too big, too... normal."

Noticing the puzzlement on Thania's face, she went on, "When certain stars approach the end of their life, the nuclear reactions inside them become insufficient to balance their gravity. They begin to shrink; their density rises until they reach a point where a cubic inch of the material would weight hundreds of tons. If they shrink any further, the atoms are crushed until they become stars composed almost entirely of neutrons."

"Once that happens, you get the total mass of a normal star compressed into one with a radius of only a few miles," Abna put in.

"And quite clearly that hasn't happened in this case." Thania nodded to indicate that she understood.

"So there has to be another rational explanation," the Amazon finished. "But at the moment, I can't think of one." She carefully placed the two spectrograms in the pocket of her suit. "I suggest we leave that particular problem for later. In the meantime, we should explore that jungle out there—and keep your weapons handy. Those sounds we heard weren't made by the wind in the trees."

On an alien planet it was unwise to take chances with anything. Animals, even the vegetation, which on the surface looked innocuous, could often turn out to be highly dangerous. The going proved to be more difficult than they had thought as they made their way towards the trees. It was not so much the ground itself but before they had gone very far, long, thin creepers covered virtually all of it.

These seemed to have a life of their own, coiling around their ankles in an attempt to hold them immobile. The Amazon threw a glance towards the edge of the jungle still almost two hundred yards away.

Exasperated, she said firmly, "It will take us an hour to get there through this vegetation." She took her protonic blaster from her belt and aimed it at the ground in front of her. Instantly, a large section of the tendrils was transformed into ash. Using their own weapons, the others proceeded to do the same, their shoes crunching in the charred remains.

Within the jungle, the silence was now absolute. Huge ferns clustered around the bases of the trees and there were large blue flowers, the heady scent of which made them momentarily giddy. But the Amazon noticed that, here and there, were narrow stretches where no vegetation grew. There was just hard-packed earth, clearly tracks that were obviously well used. They could have been merely animal tracks but she had the feeling they had been made by creatures more humanoid than beasts.

The weird howls they had picked out earlier had all fallen silent. Now however, there was a watching, waiting quality about the titan trees that caught at the Amazon's nerves. She had the feeling that hidden eyes were following their every move. Glancing round at the others, she asked, "Do you feel it too?"

Mexone nodded. "There's someone, or something, here. Whoever they are, they certainly don't mean to show themselves."

"That's what I was thinking. I don't like this at all. Everyone keep their eyes open. This is just the place for a surprise attack."

Strung out in a loose line, they walked forward, every sense alert for trouble. Very little sunlight managed to penetrate the thick branches overhead and in the deep gloom it was possible to imagine anything.

Then a sudden movement among the trees a short distance ahead immediately caught the Amazon's attention. Swiftly, she brought up the protonic blaster and squeezed the stud. A thin beam of energy speared into the shadows.

Before she could fire again, the trees around them came alive. Long, sinewy branches dropped onto the Crusaders, curling around them and pinning their arms to their sides. The blaster dropped from the Amazon's fingers as she felt the constricting branch tighten, lifting her off the ground.

From the edge of her vision, she saw that the same thing had happened to the four others.

The attack from the trees had come as a complete surprise to the Amazon but she recovered swiftly. The coiling branch squeezed inexorably until all of the air seemed to have been expelled from her lungs. Her face a mask of strain and effort, she tensed the steel muscles in her arms and shoulders until they bulged beneath the material of the suit. For a moment, it seemed that even her superhuman strength was not enough.

Then, with an explosive crack, the branch snapped in several places and fell away, releasing its hold. The Amazon fell six feet onto a thick layer of blue moss that covered the ground beneath the trees, rolled over twice and came quickly to her feet. Bending, she retrieved her blaster. Abna had already freed himself. The other three were still caught in the vise-like grip of the trees. Aiming swiftly, the Amazon swung the beam in a short arc, slicing through the tough vegetation.

Mexone and Thania had only been lifted a few feet from the ground but Viona had been swung high into the air. Now, with the branch cut through, she came tumbling across the track. Without pausing to think, the Amazon darted forward as the girl came hurtling towards her. Bracing herself, she caught the tumbling figure in her arms, lowering her gently to the ground, the encircling branch still wrapped tightly around her body. Grasping it with her yellow hands, the Amazon ripped it away with ease.

"We'd better make our way back to the clearing and away from these trees before they attack again," she called tautly. "I don't relish the idea of this entire jungle turning against us."

Once safely on board one of the pinnaces, while Viona and Thania prepared some food, the Amazon and Abna discussed the recent events.

Abna said, "At least we know this planet isn't devoid of some kind of intelligent life if you call the way those trees reacted as some kind of intelligence. Clearly they don't like intruders venturing here, Vi."

"Mmm." The Amazon pursed her lips. "Somehow, I think there's more to it than that. Did you notice that they made no move against us when we first entered the jungle? It was only after I fired at that shape I noticed among the trees that they attacked."

"You're suggesting they reacted in that way to protect whatever it was you saw?"

"It's possible. My guess is that there's some kind of symbiosis between the inhabitants of this planet and the trees. It may simply be that they protect each other. On the other hand, this strange relationship may go deeper than that. Whatever it is, it's something I'd like to find out if only to satisfy my natural scientific curiosity."

From the other side of the small cabin, Mexone asked, "Do you intend we should spend the night down here, Amazon? Wouldn't we be a lot safer back on board the Ultra?"

The Amazon gave an emphatic shake of her head. "Safer—yes, but we wouldn't learn anything. If possible, I want to question one of the natives. After all, it seems they're the only ones who can give us any information about the third planet we saw."

"Or thought we saw," Abna interjected. "We know it isn't there now and I'm still sure it was either a fault with the telescope or perhaps something to do with that invisible shield."

"And how do you think we might get our hands on one of the natives?" Viona brought food and drink over to the small table. Since it was quite crowded with the five of them there, it meant they had to eat standing up.

The Amazon smiled. Between mouthfuls, she said, "Curiosity, Viona. Simple curiosity."

"I don't understand."

"Just think. Those natives are just as curious about us as we are about them. They won't dare to approach the pinnace during daylight now they know we have weapons capable of killing them. They'll almost certainly sneak up on us once it's dark. Then we'll be ready for them."

* * * *

Twilight on the planet lasted for almost an hour but finally, the last segment of the giant blue sun dipped below the horizon. Overhead, the sky was not completely dark and from the pinnace it was possible to discern the dark shadow of the jungle some three hundred yards away. Nothing moved in the dimness.

Some twenty yards from the small vessel, the Amazon was now crouched in a deep hollow, every sense alert as she listened for any sound to break the deep, brooding silence. The remaining four Crusaders were inside the pinnace. All of the lights had been switched off enabling them to clearly observe everything outside without being seen themselves.

"Do you really think any of these natives will come?" Viona whispered in the darkness.

Peering intently through the viewing port, Abna nodded. "I agree with your mother. It's quite possible that a visit like ours from some other world has never happened here before. We've seen it on a number of planets we've landed on in the past. Where the natives are much lower down the scale of evolution, they often regard such happenings as visitations from their gods. I think they're just as curious about us as we are about them."

Ten minutes passed. Still the silence outside remained unbroken. Then Viona pointed.

"There's something there just inside the trees."

Abna glanced through the small port. Vague shapes were just visible near the jungle perimeter. In the gloom it was impossible to estimate how many there were.

A moment later, two of the shadowy figures emerged from the darkness on the edge under the tall trees. The Amazon had also been quick to spot them as she crouched down in the hollow, making herself as small as possible.

It was clear the natives were wary. From what she could see they were tall and humanoid in outline. Both held long spears in their hands, crude weapons but highly effective if they found their mark. Holding her breath, she waited. As they slowly advanced into the open, she was able to make out more details. Both were well over seven feet in height, muscular and blue-skinned. How many more were concealed among the trees she didn't know but it was doubtful if these two were alone.

Cautiously, the two natives approached the pinnace where the rest of the Crusaders were concealed. When they were about twenty feet from it one of them raised his spear and hurled it with amazing force at the vessel. It struck the side and rebounded onto the ground without making a dent in the tough metal. For a moment, they hesitated. Clearly they had expected the weapon to have had some effect.

Tensing the muscles of her legs, the Amazon waited for a second and then hurled herself forward. Taken completely by surprise, the natives spun round. In the dimness, she could see their eyes, wide and startled by her sudden appearance. The second one threw his spear at her but the Amazon was ready, expecting this move. Without pausing in her run, she twisted adroitly to one side and the weapon flew through the air without hitting its target.

Immediately, the natives turned to run back for the jungle, their long legs carrying them swiftly across the clearing. But they were no match for the Amazon. Before they had covered half the distance, she threw herself forward, catching both of them around the legs. As they fell, she delivered two swift blows with the sides of her hands to their necks.

Now she had to act quickly before there was any retaliation from others who might be hiding among the trees. Bending, she hauled their unconscious bodies upright, throwing one over each shoulder. Turning smoothly, she ran back towards the pinnace.

Behind her, a chorus of savage yells broke out. A shower of thrown spears arced through the air behind her but already she was out of their range, carrying the weight of the two inert bodies easily. By the time she reached the airlock it was already open.

Reaching down, Abna took one of the natives from her. Climbing inside, she called:

"Close the airlock. There are more of them out there and they may decide to try to rescue their friends."

Lowering her burden to the floor, she straightened. "We'd better get back to the Ultra. Then we'll secure these two and see if we can communicate with them once they come round." She glanced across at Mexone and Viona. "Both of you had better come with us rather than try to reach the other pinnace. Even though these natives seem to have only spears, it's better to be safe than sorry."

"You intend leaving it here?" Thania's raised her eyebrows in surprise.

"It'll be quite safe and we have its exact coordinates. We can pick it up any time we like."

With Abna at the controls, the pinnace blasted off from the planet, following the automatic beacon on board the Ultra where it still moved in its stable orbit. Once inside, they strapped the two natives securely into chairs and then discarded their suits. In the harsh actinic light they were able to see their captives clearly for the first time.

Both were taller than themselves, even the seven-foot Abna was appreciably shorter. Their blue skin made them appear even more alien than they really were. They were almost identically dressed in coarse tunics but apart from the pointed ears set close to their skulls, they looked remarkably humanoid.

"You're sure those chains will hold them once they regain consciousness?" Mexone asked anxiously. "Judging by their size, I'd say they could wreak some damage if they got free."

"They won't break free," the Amazon declared emphatically. "Those chains are of tetralumin. Even an elephant couldn't break them."

One of the natives stirred and opened his eyes. Larger than normal, they had a cat-like appearance with a large pupil which contracted slightly in the brilliant light.

"Evidently they're more used to the darkness of the jungle than daylight with eyes like that," Viona observed.

"So it would seem," nodded her mother.

The second native's eyes flicked open. Unlike his companion he took in at a glance what had happened for almost at once for he struggled violently against the chains that held him down. Then he uttered a stream of shrill clicking sounds, glaring wildly at his captors.

"I'll try and impress English into his brain," Abna said. "Quickest way to make progress."

Seating himself in front of the nearest native, Abna stared into his eyes. The native sat passively, apparently held in thrall. Frowning slightly in intense concentration, Abna focussed his mind, meshing it with that of the native. Through narrowed eyes, he saw the other give a sudden start, then relax. It was almost as if the native understood what he was trying to achieve. There was no mental resistance on the part of his subject as Abna had sometimes encountered in the past.

Ten minutes later, Abna straightened in his chair. "I think you'll find that he now has some command of the English language. He's not fluent but he will understand most simple concepts."

"Good." The Amazon turned to face the native. "What is your name?"

"Algar. My friend here is called Dorem."

"Okay, Algar. Just why did you attack us in the forest?"

"But it wasn't them who attacked us in the jungle," Thania interrupted. "It was the—"

The Amazon silenced her with an abrupt gesture. "It was you who made the trees try to kill us, wasn't it?"

"You fired a weapon at one of us." The words sounded strange as Algar spoke. It was as if he were trying to shape sounds that were alien to his vocal chords. "We are as one with the trees. They protect us and we do the same for them. We are part of each other's lives. We also thought you were the others come to take more of us away."

For a moment, the Amazon stared at him in surprise. Then she said harshly, "Who comes to take you away?"

"Those from the other place out there." The native turned his head as if trying to look through the hull of the Ultra—out into space.

"He either means from that third planet, or some other planetary system," Abna said.

The Amazon sat back, her full lips compressed into a hard line. She was silent for almost a minute before asking, "Do you mean from that other world of your two suns?"

The native made a movement of his head that they took for a nod of affirmation. Then he said slowly, as if searching for the right words, "The world which is sometimes there and at other times is gone."

The Amazon shook her head in bewilderment. "This gets more curious by the minute," she muttered.

"Certainly it explains what we've found," Mexone said. "That planet was there moving between these two suns when we first discovered it—but later there was no sign of it."

The Amazon placed her elbows on the table and made a pyramid of her fingers. Musingly, she said, "But it still doesn't make sense. A planet can't just disappear and then reappear. I don't believe there's any race sufficiently advanced scientifically to move an entire planet like that. Even if they could, the question is—why?"

Standing behind her mother, Viona said, "I think we'll need a lot more information from this native before we get any answer to that question. We're not even sure that what he's telling us is the truth."

"I believe he is," Abna put in. "We've already noticed the odd behavior of that planet for ourselves. Furthermore, he's got no reason to lie. What interests me at the moment is—who are these others he talks about? Quite clearly there's some other race intent on taking these people away. And from what he implies, they don't go willingly. My guess is that we've come up against interstellar slavers and if that's the case, it's up to us to put a stop to it."

As this was their main self-appointed role, he knew the others would agree—which they did instantly.

Abna turned back to Algar as a thought seemed to strike him. "These others who attack you—do they speak your language?"

The native hesitated. "Yes—in a fashion. They speak strangely to us, but our words come from a magic box they carry—"

"Obviously some kind of language translator," the Amazon interrupted impatiently. "What's your idea, Abna? We've no way of learning their oppressor's language until we actually encounter them, and—"

"We don't need to know their language," Abna smiled. "Think about it, Vi. The aliens are using these blue-skins as slaves, so they need to give them orders in their own language. So they use portable mechanical translators. They speak in their own language, and the instrument they carry repeats their words in Algar's language."

"What of it?" the Amazon asked, irritated.

"I think I know what dad's getting at," Viona put in, her eyes gleaming. "We have similar Language Translators ourselves, modified from the devices we encountered on Thania's planet. If we take a reading from Algar's brain, we can add his language to the Ultra's computer records."

"My idea exactly," Abna nodded. "It may just give us an edge when we eventually meet up with these invaders."

The Amazon shrugged. "It might—though I can't see how at the moment. Nevertheless—"

Crossing to a small cabinet, she brought out the portable Language Translator and placed it on the table directly in front of their captives.

Smiling reassuringly, she attached the sucker cables around Algar's skull. "This will only take a moment: the instrument will absorb all details of your language directly from your brain. Don't worry—it isn't painful."

Algar sat impassively as the instrument went silently to work. At length the Amazon detached the suckered cables, and picked the instrument up. Going across to the control board, she connected the instrument to the Ultra's computer.

Turning, the Amazon said briskly, "That's that. Algar's language is now stored in the Ultra's computer and linked to the ship's radio speaker, and in the language circuits of our portable translator devices. Satisfied now, Abna?"

"Perfectly."

"Then I suggest we all eat and then get some sleep."

"And what do we do with these two?" Mexone gestured towards the natives.

"I think they realize we're not their enemies and mean them no harm," she replied.

"We'll remove the chains and then lock them in one of the storerooms for the night. We then take it in turns to maintain a watch."

Thania looked puzzled. "If we lock them up, surely there's no chance they could get out."

The Amazon smiled. "We're not going to keep a watch on them, Thania. I want the region around this planet kept under constant observation. If those invaders should return, I want to know about it immediately."

CHAPTER 3

SEETEE SUN

IT was five hours later. Abna was on watch having been woken by Mexone only a few minutes earlier. There had been no trouble from the two natives after they had been taken to the storeroom, given food and drink, and provided with blankets. It seemed that both of them had now been convinced that the Crusaders were not in league with those others who carried out systematic raids on their world.

On the visiscreen, the nearby planet now showed as a bright crescent occupying almost the whole of the screen. He cast his mind back to the sequence of events that had led to the discovery of this strange stellar system. There had to be a logical answer somewhere to explain what they had found. At the back of his mind, a little thought had been nagging at him ever since that native had confirmed the odd behavior of the third planet. He tried desperately to bring it out into the open, to recognize what it was, but it continued to elude him.

Sighing, he turned the scanner through a full half-circle so that it gave an image of the region of space at their rear. Almost at once, the blue giant sun appeared. To one side of the glaring disc, he made out the gibbous disc of the largest planet. It possessed a banded appearance very much like that of his home world Jupiter where he had spent the first part of his life enclosed within the huge dome which had protected his Atlantean colony from the swirling poisonous gases of Jupiter's atmosphere.

Somehow, he doubted if this race of marauding space pirates came from that planet. Any race evolving on such a world would, unlike the inhabitants of his wife's home world, Earth, have no knowledge of the stars, being unable to see them through such a deep, turbulent atmosphere.

"Do you mind if I join you, Abna?"

Surprised, he turned swiftly in the chair to find Thania standing just behind him. There was an impish grin on her youthful features.

"I couldn't sleep. I guess I'm too excited about what we've found here." She sat down in the chair beside him, her elbows on the control panel, her chin cupped in her hands. She threw a quick glance at the screen. "What are you doing?"

"I was just trying to puzzle out this enigma about the third planet, how it can be there one minute and gone the next."

Thania remained silent for a moment, then said, "I don't suppose—" she paused uncertainly.

"Go on," Abna urged. "What were you going to say?"

"I don't know too much about these things and it's probably nothing but when we saw it from deep space, it was just beginning to pass between these two stars and—"

"That could be the answer!" Abna interrupted with a trace of excitement in his voice. "Why didn't we think of that before?" Very slowly, he adjusted the view on the screen until it showed both suns. "I think Vi should be told about this. Would you wake her and tell her it's something vitally important."

Getting up, Thania left the cabin, returning three minutes later with the Amazon.

"What is it, Abna?" the Amazon asked. "Have those raiders returned?"

Abna shook his head. "No, Vi, this is something else. There's been something nagging at my mind ever since that native confirmed the odd behavior of that planet. It was Thania who crystallized the idea in my head—the reason why that third planet keeps vanishing and then reappearing."

"You think you have the answer?"

"I'm fairly sure I have." He pointed to where the blue and yellow suns showed on the huge screen. "You remember you took a couple of spectrograms of that yellow sun out there, how it has a spectrum completely unlike anything we've come across before?"

"Of course, but we ruled out the possibility that it's a white dwarf for a neutron star."

"We did," he agreed. "But there's one other possibility we didn't consider. My guess is that this star—" he indicated the yellow component, "—is a seetee sun."

"Seetee?" Thania echoed the word with a look of incomprehension on her face.

"That's right. CT—contra-terrene. It means that it's composed of antimatter, made up of particles having the opposite electrical charge to that of those we know. They have a nucleus of antiprotons with positrons orbiting them in place of the normal protons and electrons."

The Amazon immediately recognized the logic behind his statement and pursued his idea further. "Then there must be a very strange force field operating between these two suns. You think it's one powerful enough to warp space-time to such an extent that, whenever that planet passed through it, it's thrown down a wormhole into some other dimension?"

"It's certainly the queerest situation I've ever known," Abna admitted. "Until we examined this solar system, I would've said it's impossible for such a sun to exist in our galaxy. The only explanation I can give is that it must have wandered into this region from somewhere outside the galaxy—possibly from that intergalactic gulf which lies between us and the Andromeda Nebula."

The Amazon nodded slowly. The full implications of his theory were only just beginning to sink in, but her immense scientific knowledge was already starting to slot the pieces of this cosmic jigsaw into place. This was something they had never encountered before and, as yet, the picture was not sufficiently complete for her to reach any definite conclusions. One thing, however, she was sure of.

These pirate slavers were also aware of this peculiar situation and were taking advantage of it for their own ends. They were abducting natives from that jungle planet and transporting them somewhere else and periodically returning for more. Her belief in justice for oppressed races was appalled by this.

Through tightly-clenched teeth, she said harshly, "Then if you're right, Abna, it's our duty to put a stop to what's happening here."

"And how do we do that?" Thania inquired. "We don't even know where this planet goes once it enters that force field. It could be anywhere in the galaxy."

"Or even anywhere in time," Abna added disconsolately.

"One thing still puzzles me," Thania said, frowning. "Shouldn't the appearance and disappearance of this planet cause gravitational upheavals amongst the other planets? Yet it doesn't appear to."

"As to that," Abna said slowly. "I can guess at the probable explanation. When the seetee sun originally wandered into the galaxy from the intergalactic deeps to be captured by the blue giant sun, the planet had to be a planet circling the blue giant—"

"That's right," the Amazon put in. "if it had been a planet of the seetee sun, it would also be composed of antimatter."

"Therefore," Abna resumed, "the planetary orbits must have become stabilized after the arrival of the seetee star. Whenever the planet vanishes, its gravitational effect still remains because of an oscillating resonance set up along the wormhole."

The Amazon's smile was grim and uncompromising. "Once that planet reappears, as it's bound to do considering that this process of capturing these natives seems to have been going on for some time, two of us will take a pinnace and land on the planet. Wherever it goes, we go with it."

Abna frowned. "That's taking an awfully big risk, Vi. It will mean that two of us will be completely cut off from the others. There'll be no way we can keep in contact."

"I realize that, Abna. But aren't we in the business of taking such risks? No matter what you say, my mind is made up. This evil trade in people, even if they are only just above savages on the technological level, has been going on for too long. We must put an end to it."

Abna shrugged. "All right. Then we'll go ahead with your plan but I'd feel a lot easier if we took the Ultra down to that planet. The five of us would have a better chance of survival against what might be at the other end than just two of us as you're proposing."

"And two in a small pinnace would have a far greater chance of being undetected than all of us in the Ultra."

There was no further argument. Over the next few hours a constant watch was kept for any reappearance of the third planet but without success. Wherever it had gone, it had still not returned. As trained scientists both the Amazon and Abna were aware that, although his theory explained most of the facts as they knew them, there were obvious flaws in it.

If they came into contact, matter and antimatter annihilated each other with the production of a tremendous amount of energy. Both of these suns were radiating, not only light and other forms of electromagnetic radiation, they also possessed solar winds, charged particles that were thrown out from their surfaces with terrific velocities.

Therefore, if the laws of physics held in this region of the galaxy, these particles should annihilate each other somewhere between the two suns—exactly where they had first seen this planet.

Yet quite clearly, this did not happen. There seemed to be a narrow zone where the normal laws of physics did not operate. Instead of the particles destroying each other in a blaze of hard radiation, space-time was warped to such a degree that an entire planet vanished.

So far, so good, the Amazon thought as she pondered the problem. It was well known that gravity was simply the result of space-time being curved by the presence of matter. The big stumbling block with Abna's theory was—why did the planet reappear, time after time?

Unable to find a logical reason for it, she voiced her concern to the others. "Everything else seems to fit perfectly," she said. "I've no idea why the interaction between particles of matter and antimatter should behave in this way instead of being totally destroyed—but I'm willing to admit that it's possible. But such a warp in space-time should be a one-way system."

"Why is that?" Thania asked, struggling to absorb the technical details of the conversation.

"Well we know that such wormholes through a higher dimension than our normal space-time are possible but in the past they've always been associated with black holes where the whole mass of a sun is concentrated in a single point we call a singularity. If someone could enter that singularity without being torn to pieces by the tremendous gravity, they could find themselves millions of light years away, or even in another universe. In our last adventure together, on Chameleon Planet, Abna and I encountered an alien race who actually managed the feat."

"The point Vi is trying to make," Abna put in, "is that the ends of the wormhole are in space. You cannot produce one in a laboratory on some planet. If you tried, everything in the vicinity would be automatically sucked into it. There's no proof that the other end of this wormhole will produce a parallel space warp to enable you to return here."

"You're absolutely sure that native was telling the truth when he said these raiders keep coming back for more of his people?" Viona asked. "After all, there wasn't time to give him a complete mastery of English."

"That wouldn't be necessary. It's clear that at first he thought we were members of this other race and therefore it's obvious he expected them to return."

"Then there's only one possible explanation," Abna said soberly. "There must be another system virtually identical with this one at the other end. Somehow, this wormhole through another dimension must link the two, making a return journey possible."

"That's possible, I suppose." The Amazon was not entirely convinced of this explanation. "But isn't it stretching coincidence a bit too far? I wouldn't have expected to find one seetee sun in the galaxy let alone two of them, possibly thousands of light years apart. However, in the absence of any other plausible theory, I'm willing to go along with this one."

* * * *

The Amazon took the Ultra far out in space, well beyond the giant blue sun to a position where it was possible for the scanner to take in the whole system. She judged they were also well beyond the range of any scanners the enemy fleet might have once they arrived.

By questioning the native who understood English, they found that both of them were quite willing to cooperate with the Crusaders now they knew they were there to help them. Occasionally, the two of them would talk between themselves in the odd clicking language with Algar translating what his companion said.

From their conversation, the Crusaders had ascertained that slaves were being taken from the planet, Thoron, on a regular basis and these raids had been occurring for as long as Algar could remember. Over a long period, they had also become aware of the peculiar characteristics of this third world, the name of which, when translated into English, was Uxxar. As far as they could determine, Uxxar always reappeared at the same point in its orbit as where it vanished which confirmed their theory.

Once she had assured herself that the Ultra was in a safe position, the Amazon went to look for Abna, finding him in the large library, which, apart from containing star maps of most of the galaxy, also kept the records of every planet they had visited over the years since they had begun their interstellar exploration. He was bending over the table making calculations.

He glanced up as she entered, "I've been working out how long Uxxar takes to go around that seetee sun," he said in answer to her look of mute inquiry. "The best estimate I can come up with is approximately fourteen of our days." Before she could interrupt, he went on, "I know it's unbelievable."

"Unbelievable! It's almost impossible. That's only half the time it takes the Moon to revolve around the Earth. That planet must be traveling at close on two hundred thousand miles an hour in its orbit."

"Nonetheless, that's what the figures give."

The Amazon stared down at the calculation on the table, checking them mentally. She could see no error in them, not that she expected any knowing Abna's mathematical skills. "Then we have to wait several days before Uxxar reappears in this system."

"That's right and I suggest we spend that time making preparations. This is going to be tricky and once again, I must admit I don't like the idea of just two of us landing on Uxxar, leaving the others on board the Ultra. If something goes wrong, there would be no way we could discover where in the galaxy you are. There are a hundred billion suns out there. You could be on a planet of almost any one of them."

It had already been decided that the Amazon and Mexone would take the small pinnace and land on Uxxar to follow the space pirates once that world vanished into another dimension.

The Amazon, too, was not happy with her plan but try as she would she could see no other alternative. This cruel race was a formidable one. Any civilization capable of raiding peaceful planets and taking their people into captivity had to be stopped, if not wiped out utterly.

* * * *

Abna's calculations proved to be correct. It was ten days later when Viona called the others into the control room and pointed towards the visiplate. All five leaned forward over the control panel, fixing their attention on the region between the two suns. Uxxar was there, just as they had first seen the planet, now continuing in its orbit around the yellow sun.

"I think we'll now see some action," The Amazon said with a faint smile. "This inactivity is beginning to bore me." To Abna, she went on, "Take the Ultra in closer. Mexone and Viona—check that all of the weapons are ready."

The Ultra carried a huge collection of weapons, including several large protonic blasters and a number of cannon capable of firing rockets with nuclear warheads over tremendous distances.

Several minutes passed without anything happening. Then from in front of the controls, Abna said sharply, "It seems they're about to begin their operations, Vi."

Glancing at the screen, the Amazon saw that three spaceships had lifted off from Uxxar and were climbing swiftly into space. All were of an odd angular design totally unlike the sleek lines of the Ultra. From their trajectory, it was soon evident they were heading high above the instability zone between the two suns and in the direction of Thoron.

In the light of the blue sun it was just possible to see that they were all heavily armed with various weapons of an unfamiliar shape sprouting from the hulls.

Viona said quietly, "I don't recognize any of their artillery, mother."

The Amazon frowned. "I don't honestly know why they're carrying such armament. With that barrier in place, they can't be expecting any opposition and they wouldn't encounter any other vessels within that ultra-dimensional continuum."

"So do we go after them?" Abna asked.

The Amazon watched the trio of spaceships and then said harshly, "It would seem they've spotted us and are coming after us."

Two of the alien spacecraft had suddenly altered course and were heading straight for the Ultra while the third continued on its flight towards Thoron. It was evident that the enemy possessed an extremely efficient and sensitive locating device to have discovered them so quickly, the Amazon thought as she took over the ship's controls from Abna. Without asking, she knew that the other three Crusaders were already manning the weapons.

On the screen she saw that the two enemy spaceships had separated. Whoever was in command certainly knew his job, dividing his force and preparing to attack from two directions. As they came closer, two flashes of brilliant light appeared along the side of the nearer vessel. Less than a minute later the Ultra shuddered under the force of twin explosions.

Grimly, the Amazon tightened her lips, her hands resting lightly on the controls as she braced herself, turning the vessel into a tight curve. The acceleration pulled at their bodies. Viona's voice came over the communication speaker. "They've just fired two nuclear bombs at us."

"Is there any damage?" the Amazon snapped. Immediately she had spotted the flashes, she had activated the protective screen around the entire length of the Ultra.

A pause, then Viona's answer came back. "No, there doesn't seem to be. The screen is still holding."

"Good. Then let's show them what we've got."

Retaliation was swift and accurate. Four nuclear rockets sped from the Ultra, their pencil-thin energy exhausts just visible against the blackness of space. The enemy vessel attempted to turn violently but was far too slow. One of the bombs missed its target but the remaining three struck at closely spaced intervals along its entire length. The vivid flashes were clearly visible on board the Ultra. Moments later, the entire enemy vessel disintegrated amid the violence of a massive nuclear explosion.

"What happened?" Mexone's voice echoed eerily over the communicator. "Those bombs might have crippled that vessel but they seem to have utterly destroyed it."

The Amazon replied, "My guess is that our bombs somehow triggered a chain reaction in their atomic engines. But we still have the other one to contend with. It's coming up fast on the starboard bow. Can you all see it?"

"We've got it in sight, mother." Viona's voice this time.

A second salvo of rockets speared towards the oncoming alien vessel but this time they exploded harmlessly before they hit the ship.

"They've put up some kind of protective screen around the vessel like ours," Abna said harshly. "The bombs can't pierce it."

"This one isn't going to be so easy." The Amazon muttered, not once taking her glance from the controls. "We have our own shield in place but I don't want this to end in stalemate. I want to know what's happening down on Thoron. All of you—brace yourselves, this isn't going to be pleasant."

Swiftly, she prepared to put the Ultra into the tightest curve she had ever attempted but at that moment, Viona called, "They've stopped! And so have we!"

Scarcely were the words out of her mouth than the image on the screen vanished. There was an instant of complete blackness and then another picture appeared. It was clearly the control room of the other vessel. The head and shoulders of what looked like a man, wearing some kind of uniform, occupied most of the screen but although he was humanoid in apparent size and shape, that was where the resemblance stopped.

The features were more like those of a reptile than a mammal; a long, out-thrusting snout and a mouth filled with pointed teeth. The skull was elongated with small ears and the forehead flat. The eyes that stared at them from the screen were lidless, showing no trace of emotion.

The being spoke in a hissing voice that was as cold as it was unintelligible. His words were immediately followed by a second mechanical voice speaking in Agar's language. Then the Ultra's computer reproduced the words in English.

"Who are you? Where do you come from?"

Without taking her gaze off the image, the Amazon said harshly: "We are known as the Cosmic Crusaders. We come from a sun so far away you would not be able to see it."

There was a pause while her words were translated into Algar's language and then back into the alien's own language at his end, and the creature absorbed what she had said. Then the ice-cold voice resumed, and the translation came from the Ultra's radio speakers.

"Before we destroy you and your vessel, you will answer our questions, otherwise we will blast your spaceship out of space. How did you get here past the screen we put up? What are you doing in this area?"

"We are merely exploring the galaxy," the Amazon replied. She knew she had to keep talking while she figured out a way of escape from this tight situation. If these creatures could erect such a vast and impenetrable screen as that which they had encountered, it was likely their weapons were also more powerful than any they had on board the Ultra. It seemed to have been pure luck they had succeeded in destroying that other vessel either that; or those on board that doomed ship had not had sufficient time in which to erect their protective shield.

"Exploring—or trying to interfere in what is happening here?" the cruel voice went on.

"We are—" the Amazon began but she was interrupted before she could say anything more.

"There is no point in lying to us. We have already scanned your ship for all life forms. We know there are five of your race on board, together with two of the natives from the planet they call Thoron. Clearly you know far too much and we have no intention of allowing you to interfere with our plans."

"So you mean to kill us. Is that how you treat other civilized races you come across in the galaxy?"

"Any race we Vorans regard as being sufficiently advanced to represent a threat to us, we eliminate. Others we take as slaves to work for us on our own world."

Abna suddenly reached out and switched off the Language Translator. "We can talk freely now; they don't understand English," he explained. He looked at the Amazon. "It's clear they mean what they say, Vi. We've only two chances of getting out of this. Either we use the invisibility device, or we risk going into hyperspace and hope they can't follow us there."

The Amazon knew she had to make up her mind within the next minute. There was no pity, no hint of compassion, in the reptilian features of the Voran. She had met races like this before; cruel beings whose only aim was complete domination and the extinction of any race posing a threat to them.

Both options open to them carried grave risks. There would be no time in which to plot a course into the Ultra's computer for a trip through hyperspace and she had no idea whether the Voran spaceship possessed any form of hyperdrive. If it did, and they also had some tracking device that operated in hyperspace, such a course would achieve nothing. That vessel could hunt them down as easily as in normal space. Furthermore, she did not know what effect hyperspace might have on the two natives they had with them. At the moment her plan was to keep them as allies once they landed again on Thoron.

She made her decision and prayed it would be the right one. Moving her left arm very slowly so that it would not be noticed by the alien on the other vessel, she threw the switch on the control panel. Energy flowed through the entire vessel, shifting the electron orbits in the atoms that made up the Ultra into a different sideways pattern.

All around them there now seemed to be nothing but empty space. From the corner of her eye, she saw Thania slump against the invisible wall of the ship as vertigo threatened to send her spinning. She knew just how the girl was feeling at that moment. The impression of being suspended above millions of light years of absolute nothing could be unnerving even for those who had experienced it before. Thania had known it once but then she had been partially prepared for it.

The Amazon had a moment in which to see the astonished expression on the Voran commander's features as the Ultra abruptly disappeared from their screens. Then the atomic engines gave a deep-throated roar as she increased their power. Acceleration pulled at them as she turned the Ultra into a tight curve, heading for the giant sun.

"Everyone keep an eye on that spaceship," she called urgently. "It won't take them long to figure out what's happened and I've no doubt they have matter detectors with them. Then they'll come after us."

CHAPTER 4

UXXOR

AN hour later, the Ultra was still in orbit around the blue giant sun. So far there had been no sign of the pursuing enemy vessel. Either the Voran commander had been unable to determine in which direction they had gone, or had believed they had somehow fled away from the region, realizing they had come up against a force more powerful than their own.

The Amazon knew the Vorans would not give up searching for them. While they remained in this solar system they were an unknown quantity, a definite menace to their operations. She had no idea what kind of weapons and instruments were on board the Voran spaceship. With their advanced technology, it was possible they had matter scanners that could cover this entire system of suns and planets, able to pick them out over vast distances.

Once she was certain the enemy vessel was nowhere in sight, however, the Amazon reversed the energy flow through the ship and they found themselves standing on solid metal once more.

"So what do we do now?" Viona asked. "At least we know something of this warlike race we're up against."

"True," the Amazon said musingly, "but not enough."

"Well, we're fairly certain they don't originate in this solar system." Mexone put in. "As Abna can tell you, they don't come from that large planet. It would be impossible for any reptilian race to evolve there."

"And since we know they're taking these natives to some other planet which must exist at the other end of this dimensional wormhole, they're not indigenous to that world."

The Amazon nodded. "That is why I think it's important we should examine Uxxar together before it disappears again." For the moment she had discarded her original plan to go to Thoron. "Somehow, I have the feeling that is the last place the Vorans will think of looking for us."

"And you're still going ahead with your plan that you and Mexone will remain on Uxxar once it enters the wormhole?" Viona asked, a look of anxiety on her face. "If something goes wrong and you're captured, you realize they won't hesitate to kill both of you."

The Amazon gave a faint smile. "I understand your feelings for Mexone, Viona—and for me. I would feel the same for Abna if the positions were reversed." She shrugged slightly. "But when we formed the Cosmic Crusaders it was with the intention of helping and uplifting any oppressed races we found in our journeying through the galaxy. We can't give up that ideal just because there's a chance we might be killed."

"Of course we can't," Viona said after a short pause. "Perhaps I was just being selfish and thinking only of myself."

"It's perfectly understandable." The Amazon laid a slim hand on her daughter's arm. "But we're not dead yet—not by a long way. Now, let us see if we can find a suitable landing placed on Uxxar."

Swinging in a wide curve around the huge sun, they set a course for Uxxar, just visible as a bright crescent close to the rogue seetee sun. Viewing it on the screen, the Amazon thought— It looks so normal, so like Sol that it could be Sol's twin brother. But she knew, as they all did, that the antimatter of which it was composed could annihilate the Ultra and themselves in a blaze of hard radiation within microseconds if they came into contact with it.

The space around Uxxar looked completely empty as they approached the planet with no sign of any enemy vessels in the vicinity. The instruments on board the Ultra indicated—that, like Thoron, its atmosphere was breathable. In its general appearance, the surface did not differ much from Thoron.

Only one large stretch of water was visible but there were several large lakes and a multitude of rivers. Much of the land, however, seemed to be arid desert. There was no sign of large forests as they had found on Thoron. From its appearance it seemed to be an older world than Thoron.

At the controls, the Amazon said quietly, "I'll put the Ultra into a stable decelerating orbit at twelve thousand miles. That should give us a chance to study the surface thoroughly before we land. Knowing that the Vorans use it as their base, I don't want any nasty surprises once we go out onto the surface."

They entered the atmosphere on the night side of the planet, gliding smoothly through the upper layers. It was, then that the Amazon noticed that the Ultra was descending more rapidly than she had anticipated. Swiftly, she turned her attention to the instruments.

"That's odd," she remarked. "This planet seems to have a much higher gravity that I would have expected from its Earth-like appearance." She swiftly applied more power to the engines to compensate for their rate of descent.

"Then either it has a very large metallic core, or—" Mexone broke off in mid-sentence as if unsure whether to continue.

"Or it's an artificial world," Abna finished, evidently guessing at Mexone's thoughts.

"That's something we don't know." The Amazon said grimly. "We do know that the Vorans are possibly far more advanced in technological and scientific achievement than we are." Pursing her lips into a thoughtful frown, she went on, "And there's another thing. Unless I'm mistaken, this planet always turns the same hemisphere towards that seetee sun out there—rather like Mercury."

"Mercury?" Thania asked. "That hell-planet we crashed on in your solar system?"

The Amazon nodded. "Mercury orbits Sol in about eighty-eight days and being so close it's locked in its orbit. It rotates on its axis in the same time it takes to go around Sol. The sunward hemisphere is extremely hot while the other is almost at absolute zero. Not a very nice place, as you'll recall. I think we have the same thing here—though without the temperature extremes—and it could also explain Uxxar's extremely high orbital velocity. It's like a stone in a sling being whirled around by the gravitational force of this sun."

Now she understood Uxxar's peculiar characteristics, the Amazon was able to keep the Ultra on a stable course through the atmosphere. Down below them, much of the surface was ocean but the scanners soon picked up a large island that was clearly mountainous. On the infra-red screen, details of the rugged landscape showed with amazing clarity. Near the center of the island was a smooth, flat plain some ten miles in diameter, in the middle of which several bright lights were visible.

"That could be the Voran base," Thania said excitedly.

The Amazon nodded. "Since we saw nothing of any size on the sunward side when we approached Uxxar earlier, I'd say you're right."

Turning to her husband, she went on, "Well, Abna, should we land and take a closer look?"

Abna studied the rugged terrain for almost a minute before replying. "Since we've no idea when those two Voran spaceships might return with their first batch of prisoners, I suggest someone remains on board the Ultra while the others investigate. That way, we won't be taken by surprise."

"Agreed." Without any further conversation, the Amazon slowed the great spaceship still further before bringing it to rest on the plain less than a mile from the lights they had seen.

Leaving Mexone on board, the others made their way through the airlock and down onto the plain. All four were equipped with infra-red vision enabling them to see details clearly in the darkness. The lights surrounded a huge square building almost a mile long and now they were on the ground they saw that other lights showed through square windows.

The walls rose high out of the smooth plain. There were no exterior decorations and no obvious track leading up to it but the Amazon had the feeling that it had been used often in the past but not for very long intervals.

"This must be where the Vorans keep those natives until Uxxar disappears into that inter-dimensional wormhole." Viona remarked.

"Obviously," Abna said. "My guess is that at the moment it's empty. But there is a chance they may have posted guards."

"Is that likely?" the Amazon said thoughtfully. "After all, they must have been carrying out these unlawful activities for some time. Until they spotted us in space, they'd believe that no one could pass their barrier and enter this region of the galaxy. However, keep your blasters ready just in case I'm wrong."

There was no sound as they approached the side of the building. Abna threw an appraising glance at the lights on top of the tall columns. Clearly, unless these people had a generator running somewhere inside, they were not powered by electricity.

Rounding the corner of the building, they spotted the large rectangular opening two hundred yards away. Pressing themselves close against the wall, they edged their way along it, the Amazon in the lead. Reaching the edge of the huge doorway, she risked a quick look inside.

There was no movement as far as she could see and turning, she signaled to the others to follow her. In single file they moved into the building. Abna had expected to find it empty, merely a place to keep the Thoron natives on a temporary basis until they reached wherever that wormhole led. He soon discovered that he was mistaken.

One side of the huge building was occupied by what were clearly cells in which the unfortunate captives were clearly kept. There seemed to be hundreds of these. The other side, however, was filled halfway to the ceiling with machines and instruments which none of them recognized. Snaking coils and levers sprouted in all directions forming a maze of metal that was both confusing and utterly alien.

The Amazon examined them with a critical eye; then shook her head. "It's difficult to tell whether these machines are for offensive purposes or are used, in some way, to power the lights and any other energy requirements they have," she said finally. "But—"

She broke off sharply as a sudden sound came from somewhere close by. There was the clatter of heavy boots on the floor and six Voran guards appeared from between two of the huge machines. All had weapons in their hands. One of them gave a sudden shout and pointed towards the Crusaders.

A sizzling beam of intense heat speared past the Amazon's head as she instinctively threw herself sideways. Swiftly, the Crusaders spread out, diving for cover behind the machines.

"They've got us pinned down," Abna said softly. "We can't move without running into their fire."

"Just keep them occupied." Viona thrust her weapon back into her belt and motioned to Thania, her right hand pointing towards the top of the nearby machine. Reaching up, she grasped two projections and pulled herself up easily. Hand over hand, she climbed towards the top. Beside her, the teen-ager did likewise.

A heat beam flashed past the opening and drew a line of scorched, dripping metal along the front of the machine. Thrusting her protonic blaster around the edge, the Amazon squeezed the stud twice. A high-pitched scream of pain came from one of the guards.

Reaching the top of the machine, Viona crawled forward with Thania just behind her. Here, the metal was smooth and it was possible for them to move without making a sound. At the edge, she moved her head forward an inch at a time until she was able to look down. One of the guards lay sprawled on the floor where the beam from the Amazon's blaster had hit him in the chest. The other five were directly below them. None of them looked up, clearly expecting no attack from that direction.

Smoothly, Viona got her legs under her, paused for a moment and then dropped onto the shoulders of one of the Vorans. The guard's legs buckled under the impact, knocking him to the floor. Before he could recover from his surprise and bring up his weapon, she hauled him upright, got her hands under him and lifted him high over her head. Twisting slightly from the waist, she threw him at two of the other guards as they turned to meet the unexpected attack.

Both Vorans went down as the heavy body collided with them, their weapons falling from their hands. Turning to help Thania she saw that her aid wasn't needed. Both Vorans was struggling helplessly in her grip. A moment later, the Amazon came running up with the others. She gave a brisk nod of approval.

"What do we do with them now?" Thania asked. "We can't just leave them here."

The Amazon took the small portable language translator from her belt. "First, I mean to question them. There are some things I want to know." Her initial instinct had been to kill them all. She had no qualms about killing such evil, cruel creatures. They were not even human. But that could come later depending upon any answers she got.

She motioned towards the guard Viona had thrown with such ease at the others. "Get him on his feet and I'll take a reading from his brain with this instrument. Hold him steady whilst I attach the leads to his head."

Viona moved forward so quickly that the Voran was unaware of her intentions. Within seconds, she was standing behind him, her arms around him, pinning his arms to his sides.

The snarling features exhibited what appeared to be an expression of sardonic amusement at the idea that a mere slip of a girl could restrain him. Within the sleeves of his tunic, bulging muscles showed as he exerted all of his strength to free himself. But strong as they were, his muscles were no match for Viona's.

The Amazon affixed the delicate sucker-like tendrils to his head as Viona held the Voran tightly from behind.

"My instrument is linked directly to the Ultra's computer," the Amazon said. "It will scan the Voran language directly from his brain, and back to the Ultra. The Ultra's computer will then program the settings on my translator to automatically convert his language into English..." She carefully adjusted the minute controls. "...And it will also convert our speech to his."

After a few minutes a red light glowed on the instrument, signifying that the transfer had been completed.

"Good. Now let's see if he's willing to talk." To the Voran, the Amazon said harshly, "We have already destroyed one of your spaceships. When are the other two due back here with those slaves you're taking from Thoron?"

The guard made no immediate reply, then as the Amazon's words were mechanically repeated from the small speaker in his own language, his cruel reptilian eyes glared malevolently at her.

The Amazon waited for a few moments, then shrugged negligently and motioned to Viona. The girl understood at once. Tightening her arms, she squeezed his chest, forcing all of the air from his lungs.

The long, pointed jaw fell open as his breath gushed from his mouth. Stepping up to him, the Amazon said in a deceptively soft voice, "Now I'll repeat my question. When are the other spaceships due to return? If you don't answer me truthfully, Viona will either break your ribs or your back and I can assure you she's strong enough to do either."

Pause whilst the words were converted. Then, uttering a gasping snarl, the Voran grunted a reply. The translation came: "Another two hours. When they do, they'll destroy all of you."

The Amazon gave a cold, calculating smile. "We'll see about that when the time comes."

"You won't get away," the translator resumed. "Even if you try to escape, it's impossible. Knowing you were in this system, our commander has acted quickly. The barrier has now been altered so that nothing can pass through it, not even in hyperspace."

Keeping her face expressionless so as not to betray her apprehension at that remark, the Amazon thought that over. There seemed no point in the Voran lying about it. It certainly presented a problem for them. Then, with an effort, she pushed the worrying thought from her mind. There were other, more pressing, matters to attend to at the moment.

"Where do you go when this planet disappears from this solar system?" she demanded. "Back to your own world?"

"Of course." The Voran tried to appear defiant in front of his companions standing in a small group, covered by the other Crusaders. The Amazon guessed that his male ego had received a severe jolt at being overpowered by a girl.

"And where is that? Obviously you don't belong to this world."

The Voran uttered a word but the translator remained silent. Clearly it was one that the Ultra's computer had no English equivalent for. Whether it was an oath or the name of his home planet, the Amazon couldn't tell. She switched the language translator off and returned it to her belt.

"I don't think we'll get anything more out of him," she said. "But at least we have a little time to get rid of these creatures and take a good look around this place."

Before she could say any more, three of the guards broke away, ignoring the blasters trained on them, and commenced to run for the end of the building. Without any hesitation, the Amazon swung her weapon and pressed the stud three times without apparently taking any aim. All three Vorans threw up their arms and then fell forward onto their faces, lying motionless on the smooth floor.

The one still held by Viona now struggled fiercely, trying to break the girl's hold but her steel grip was immovable and finally, he gave up the attempt. The remaining Voran had clearly hoped to take advantage of his companions' abrupt movement to make a try for Abna's weapon. Now he too lay on the floor, his neck broken.

"Now we just have this one to deal with," Abna remarked. "If we let him go, he'll certainly warn the others when they get back."

Nodding, the Amazon said, "Kill him. These creatures are clearly evolved from reptiles. They don't have a spark of common decency or humanity in them."

"But—" Viona began.

The next moment, the Voran twisted sideways with a violent heave that took the girl completely by surprise. Caught off balance, she fell sideways with the guard on top of her. She still had her grip on him but with a sudden savage movement, the Voran jerked his scaled head back, hitting her with a vicious blow to the face. The impact of the hard reptilian flesh brought a sharp spasm of excruciating pain, forcing her to release her grip.

Rolling away from her, the guard made a dive for the weapon on the floor where he had dropped it. His claw-like fingers were closing around it when Abna stepped forward. The blond giant lowered his blaster and fired a single shot. At his feet, the guard twitched once and then lay still.

"Get them all out of sight," the Amazon ordered. "Then we'll take a look around before we make our getaway."

The removal of the bodies was a matter of only a few minutes. Each of the Crusaders took one of the Vorans across their shoulders and carried them to the narrow space between the huge machines and the wall.

As the Amazon brought the last one, she said, "My guess is that this building and everything in it has been here for a long time. It's possible that when the Vorans made their first exploratory journey here, they weren't sure of the kind of reception they'd get so they took no chances."

"You think these machines are weapons of some kind?" Thania asked. From the sound of her voice it was clear she had never seen anything like them.

"That would be my opinion too." Abna replied to her question. He was standing in front of one of the largest machines, intently studying what seemed to be a control panel on the front.

There was an intricate array of buttons and levers with a strange symbol beside each.

Standing beside him, the Amazon mused, "Not knowing the Voran alphabet, we'll never be able to read those characters. My guess would be that they're force field generators of some kind."

"You mean like those on Karg that they used to nullify the Ultra's atomic engines?" Thania had already seen those in action.

"Exactly."

Thania's face bore a look of alarm. "Then if they are, oughtn't we to destroy them before the Vorans decide to use them against us?"

The Amazon rubbed a hand across her forehead. "Somehow, I don't think that would be an easy thing to do. We could use the weapons on board the Ultra to wipe out this entire building and everything in it but that doesn't fit in with my plans."

"Which are that you and Mexone go with Uxxar when it disappears into that wormhole," Viona said. She rubbed her shoulder when the Voran guard had fallen on it.

"That's right. Only I've also decided to take Algar with us if he's willing to go."

Abna's brow creased. "Why take Algar?"

"Because once we arrive at wherever this inter-dimensional tube ends there are certain to be hundreds of his people held as slaves there. It's just possible that with his help we may be able to free them and turn them against the Vorans."

"You seem to have thought of everything." Abna said. "Except that those Thoron natives will be totally unarmed and I doubt if they know how to use the Vorans' weapons even if you could lay our hands on any."

The Amazon pursed her lips. "I realize how much the odds are stacked against us, Abna. But I don't intend to do nothing and let these natives rot on some planet under these cruel masters."

After a further examination of the large machines that revealed no indication of their purpose or operation, they made their way back to the Ultra.

"Did you find anything of value in there?" Mexone asked, turning away from the viewing screen. "There's been no activity here, no sign of those two Voran spaceships."

"We ran into a little trouble with six Voran guards," the Amazon said casually. "It was nothing we couldn't handle. But that building is full of machines. Unfortunately, we could make neither head nor tail of the controls." She hurried to the control board. "We'll take the Ultra out into deep space but close enough to keep Uxxar under observation. Then we switch off everything but the life support systems. That way, those two Voran spaceships may not discover us."

"Is there something in particular you're looking for?" Mexone inquired.

"If my guess is correct, those two ships will be arriving soon with their first cargoes of slaves. I'm just wondering what they'll do when they discover six of their guards are missing."

"Somehow, I don't think they're fools. They'll put two and two together and—"

"Come up with the answer that we've been there," the Amazon finished dryly. "I doubt if that will interfere with their operations on Thoron and it's a fact they can't leave this system until Uxxar passes directly between those two suns."

"Which won't happen for another five or six days if my calculations are correct." Abna focused the viewing screen onto the black gulf that separated them from the Andromeda Nebula as he spoke.

Two minutes later, the engines fired, lifting them smoothly from the plain. The lights surrounding the Voran base fell away swiftly behind them and then vanished completely—as they passed through the atmosphere and out into space.

CHAPTER 5

INTO THE WORMHOLE

FOR five days, the Cosmic Crusaders played cat and mouse with the two Voran vessels although, for the time being, it seemed the Vorans were concentrating on transferring shiploads of the natives from Thoron to Uxxar rather than searching for them.

Pacing up and down the vast control room, the Amazon fidgeted and fumed at the inactivity. She had put her plan to Algar and found the native only too willing to accompany her. In spite of the danger, his main desire now was to help his people and, if possible, put an end to this evil that had fallen upon Thoron.

Most of the time, he spent standing disconsolately with Dorem, knowing that more and more of his friends were being abducted and taken by force from their homes. Watching him, the Amazon knew instinctively that he would do everything she asked of him, even if it meant his death on some planet thousands, or millions, of light years away.

Taking up their posts in front of the visiscreen, the other Crusaders took turns to keep a watch on the Voran spaceships. At times, the Amazon wondered why neither of the enemy vessels made any determined effort to look for them. The only conclusion she could reach was that the Voran knew they could not escape from this sector of space and they intended to wait for the Ultra to come to them.

When she put this possibility to Abna, he considered it for a moment and then nodded in agreement. "I think you're right but there's no way we can get into the minds of these creatures," he said. "Since they've obviously evolved from some form of reptile, their minds and reasoning processes are completely alien to us. It would be like you trying to figure out what an intelligent lizard would do in certain circumstances."

The Amazon glanced at the small chronometer on her wrist. "There are only a few hours left before Uxxar enters that unstable zone between the suns. I'm calling a council of war so that everyone knows what's expected of them."

Five minutes later everyone, including the two natives, was seated around the large table. Since it was her plan, the Amazon began the discussions.

"In a short time," she began, choosing her words carefully, "Uxxar will pass directly between those two very dissimilar suns and disappear from this system. Together with Mexone and Algar, I intend to be on that planet when it happens."

"And the rest of us?" Viona asked.

"You remain on board the Ultra and wait for our return. Hopefully, by then, I should know exactly where this other world lies. I also hope that with Algar's help, we can find some way of freeing and arming those hundreds of natives being held captive there."

"That won't be easy," Thania said from across the table. "And how do the three of you intend to land on Uxxar without being seen? The Vorans would spot the Ultra long before it entered the atmosphere."

"I'm taking the small pinnace we still have on board. My aim is to land on that island among those mountains, out of sight from the building we found. As it's always on the night side, it might not be too difficult to do that without being observed." She glanced obliquely at Abna. "As the pinnaces have only a limited range, it will mean you'll have to take the Ultra close to Uxxar. It will be a tricky procedure. I don't want this ship caught in the space warp so you'll have to approach the planet from behind in its orbit." Inwardly, she did not doubt Abna's ability to handle the Ultra almost as well as she did herself. But this was a procedure they had never attempted before and there were a thousand things that could go wrong. Everything would have to be carried out with precision and perfect timing.

To Viona she said, "Has there been any activity in the vicinity of Thoron recently?"

Viona shook her head, her copper hair gleaming in the actinic light. "Both Voran vessels left Thoron about two hours ago heading for Uxxar. I'd say they've made their last trip on this occasion."

"Good. That means they'll be landing on Uxxar within the next hour. Then we go in." Rising lithely to her feet, she picked up her belt from the table, strapped it on; then checked that everything was there.

"Both Mexone and I are taking ultraradios with us. We'll contact you as soon as we land on that island and maintain communication with you for as long as possible."

"We'll keep listening out," Viona promised. "It's going to be a little dull not having you around and with only those natives on Thoron for company."

Algar spoke a few words to Dorem in his own tongue; then said, "You will have no trouble with my people if you land on Thoron. Dorem will explain to them that you are friends."

By the time the tiny pinnace had been readied for its journey, Abna had lined up the Ultra with Uxxar now speeding in its orbit towards the midpoint between the suns. The brilliant glare of the blue giant sun illuminated the control room.

"Everything ready?" He spoke directly into the small ultraradio.

The Amazon's voice came over loud and clear. "All three of us are securely strapped in, Abna."

"I'm now lining up the Ultra so as to approach the planet directly above the ocean. Don't forget that you'll now be clearly visible to the Vorans when you descend. That blue sun is almost directly overhead on that side of the planet now."

"I'll bear that in mind. At least, we won't be easy to spot against that glaring disc."

At Abna's side, Viona said, "Take care of yourself, Mother—Mexone. We'll all be watching for you when you return."

His hands resting on the controls, Abna turned the huge vessel into a shallow curve. Directly in front of him, Uxxar was now a large disc, one hemisphere bathed in the blue light of the giant sun, the other a faint yellow from the glow of its companion. Through the blanket of cloud that covered the ocean, he caught brief glimpses of the solitary island.

A moment later, he depressed the button that opened the outer airlock inside which the small safety machine was housed. Viona had hurried to one of the transparent ports in the side of the Ultra. After a moment, she called, "They're on their way, Abna."

Abna picked out the tiny craft heading towards the planet's atmosphere a few seconds later. Then, with an almost savage movement, he thrust forward the main engine lever. The Ultra leapt forward as the power to the engines was increased and the great ship pulled sharply away from the planet.

They were still heading into the void when the Amazon's voice came from the ultraradio. "We've landed safely on a small plateau just inside that mountain range. I don't think we were seen although there's a lot of activity just outside that building. Both of the Voran spaceships are here but they are—"

"What's wrong, Vi?" Abna scarcely realized he was shouting the words.

Then the Amazon's voice came back but now it was beginning to break up as a rush of intense static threatened to drown out her words. "Those two spaceships, Abna. They're taking off at high speed. They're... not... remaining... on the... planet! Take care, it... seems they... mean... to—"

The Amazon's voice ceased abruptly, cut off in mid-sentence. For a moment, Abna couldn't think what could have happened. Then a quick glance at the viewing screen told him the reason. Uxxar had gone!

* * * *

Even though he had been expecting it, Abna felt a distinct shock as he stared at the completely empty space between the suns where Uxxar had been just moments before. Then he pushed the thought from his mind as his keen sight picked out the two gleaming metal dots heading in their direction.

"I think we'd better get out of here as quickly as possible," he said tersely. "Those two Voran vessels look as if they mean business this time." To Thania, he added, "Better strap Dorem into one of the couches. He isn't used to this kind of acceleration."

Once this had been done, he turned the Ultra in a tight curve and headed out into the void, feeding as much power as he dared to the atomic engines. Very soon, it was apparent that fast as they were, the enemy ships were no match for the Ultra when it came to speed. Within minutes they were no more than tiny dots in the far distance.

"Where are we headed?" Viona asked after a long silence. "With the armaments the Vorans have, I doubt if there's anywhere safe for us in this solar system."

"That's just what I was thinking. We can't spend the next fourteen days simply wandering through space hoping to keep them off our tail. By the end of that time, our supply of copper would be running dangerously low."

"What about Thoron? Algar said that Dorem would tell those natives we're not the enemies they thought we were."

"That's a possibility," Abna agreed. "But now that's the first place they'll look for us. If they should attack from space while the Ultra is still on the ground we wouldn't stand much of a chance against them."

"Then what about that third planet out there?" Thania pointed to where the banded disc of the large gas planet hung against the black background of space.

Abna shook his head. "I spent much of my life on a planet like that, Thania, but no one could live there unless they were inside a pressurized dome on the surface. In addition the high gravity and atmospheric pressure down there would make things very uncomfortable for us if we had to stay inside the Ultra."

"And we won't find copper there," Viona explained to her.

"Then where else can we go while we wait for Uxxar to reappear?"

Abna said: "It's likely there could be other planetary systems not far from here. There must be at least forty suns enclosed inside that Voran barrier."

"I'll check the star maps," Viona said, turning on her heel.

Thania went to help her. For the first time since becoming the fifth Cosmic Crusader she was beginning to appreciate the vastness of the galaxy. Even so, the thought of all those hundreds of billions of suns made her head reel a little. All her life had been spent in that town on Karg where she had not given much thought to what lay beyond her own world. Now she was out in space where distances were so vast she could scarcely comprehend them.

"The nearest sun is just over ten light years away," Viona called.

"Link the telescope to the screen and used the highest magnification possible," Abna answered. "We daren't go too far in case we hit the other side of the Voran shield. At the moment we've no idea where it is in this direction. If you can, get me a spectrum of that sun at the same time."

After checking the position of the sun in question, Viona crossed to the far end of the control panel and flicked down a couple of switches. Immediately the image on the visiscreen vanished. In its place was the bright disc of the distant sun. At the very bottom of the screen appeared the spectrum, a band of colors crossed by numerous dark lines.

Abna studied it for a few moments; then nodded. "Very like our own sun but the surface temperature is about a thousand degrees higher. Stars like this normally have a retinue of planets around them."

"You're right, Abna," Thania said excitedly. She pointed. "I can see at least eight of them."

"Then we'll make for that system and hope those Voran space-ships don't follow us." Abna set the controls and then sat back in his chair. "Since we'll be traveling in hyperspace, we can be there and back in good time for Uxxar's reappearance. Make sure you're strapped into your chairs. It's just possible the enemy will come searching for us in hyperspace and I wouldn't like to be floating against the ceiling if they do and decide to attack."

* * * *

In the control room of the small pinnace, the Amazon had just watched the two Voran spaceships lift off from the open area in front of the huge building. It was something she had not expected. She had thought that all of the enemy would return to their home planet now that they had a full cargo of slaves.

The only conclusion she could reach was that the Vorans consid-ered them such a threat to their operations that they had decided to remain in this solar system until they had eliminated them and the Ultra. Whatever the reason, she knew she had to alert Abna and the others.

Clicking on the ultraradio, she sent out her warning message. The next instant she sensed the change. Everything around her vanished in a microsecond of time. There was a wrench that seemed to twist every atom and molecule in her body. She could not see, hear or feel anything. It was as if she were suspended completely alone in an utter blackness in which strange fluxes of energy coiled and spun around her.

How long the weird sensation lasted she could not tell for here—wherever here was—there was no indication of time. Like space, time had no meaning in this odd dimension.

She knew Mexone and Algar were somewhere close by, just beside her, but none of her senses could detect them. They could be a million light years away for all she knew.

Then abruptly, without any prior warning, she was back in the pinnace again, her hands resting lightly on the controls. She sucked in a deep breath and tried to clear her vision. Her eyes seemed oddly unfocussed.

Swallowing hard, she turned to look at Mexone. From the expression on his face she knew he had undergone exactly the same experience. Algar looked as if he had been to hell and back, not understanding anything of what had happened.

Forcing a wry grin, Mexone said hoarsely, "So that's what it's like—traveling in that extra dimension."

Nodding, the Amazon replied, "It's not something I'd like to go through very often." Drawing herself upright, she glanced through the port. Down below them was the huge building housing the slaves and, presumably, a number of guards. In the sky overhead hung the large disc of a blue-white sun while in the other direction was a yellow sun, smaller and horribly familiar.

The sight stunned the Amazon so much that for a full two minutes she found herself unable to speak. When she did there was sheer disbelief in her tone. "We're in exactly the same place as when we left!"

"But that's impossible." Mexone stared at the scene, his eyes wide with amazement. "There's no doubt we passed through that wormhole. It can't have brought us back to where we started. That doesn't make any sense at all."

The Amazon shook her head in perplexity. "This is something beyond my understanding at the moment. There must be a rational explanation but I can't think of one."

Mexone made to speak but at that moment something caught his attention and he pointed urgently. Three of the strange angular spaceships had appeared over the island. Already, they were dropping down through the atmosphere, braking rockets flaring as they reduced their velocity.

The two Crusaders and Algar watched intently as they landed in a wide triangular formation in front of the building. The roar of the engines ceased and a few moments later their airlocks flipped open and extending ladders appeared. Several Vorans climbed down from each and entered the building.

"Now we're sure of one thing," the Amazon said tautly. "Uxxar isn't their home planet. Clearly they come from some other system."

"That being so," Mexone remarked dryly, "how do we follow them? The pinnace isn't designed for interstellar travel."

"That problem had occurred to me. Our only chance is to get on board one of those spaceships before they blast off and conceal ourselves until they reach their destination. At the moment, I'm convinced they don't know we're here."

Mexone eyed her in amazement. "That won't be easy. In fact, I'd go so far as to say it's impossible. We'd have to cross all of that open space down there and then climb one of those ladders, all in full view of anyone inside that building."

"Can you suggest anything better?"

Mexone couldn't and a moment later he followed the Amazon through the airlock, lowering himself onto the rocks. Algar leapt the distance easily, landing on his feet like a cat. Here they were hidden from anyone on the plain by a huge slab of stone.

Taking the ultra-strong nylon cord from her belt, the Amazon looped one end over a pointed spur of rock and then began to descend, hand over hand, down the side of the sheer rock. Without pausing, Mexone and Algar followed. At any second they expected to hear a shout from the building to indicate they had been seen. But their luck held and soon they were crouched at the bottom of the rocks. Giving a dexterous flick to the cord, the Amazon unlooped it from the rock above them and returned it to her belt.

"Now comes the most dangerous part," the Amazon whispered. "I suspect they're removing Algar's friends from those cells and shackling them together. Run for the nearest spaceship. I'll go up first in case there are any guards waiting just inside the airlock. Whatever you do, don't stop either of you and don't look back. Are you ready?"

"As ready as I ever will be. I still think this is suicidal."

"Just do it. If they do spot us and open fire, we'll give a good account of ourselves."

Tensing themselves, Mexone and Algar waited until the Amazon gave the signal.

Swiftly, they sprinted across the open ground, running as fast as they had ever run. Fast as they were, the Amazon reached the bottom of the ladder leading up to the airlock a couple of feet ahead of them.

Without pausing or looking around, she commenced to climb. Grasping the metal sides, Mexone followed. At the forefront of his mind was the fear that they would never make it, that at any second, the beam from some weapon would kill them all before they reached the top.

But reach it they did. Above him, Mexone saw the Amazon pull herself swiftly into the airlock. Thrusting himself inside with Algar just behind him, he had only a second to realize there was a Voran standing only a few feet from the Amazon. Swiftly, he reached for the protonic blaster in his belt but it was not needed.

Before the guard could move and recover from his astonishment, the Amazon's right fist connected with his jaw. The blow was sufficient to break his neck before he could utter a single sound. The Amazon caught the body of the guard before he fell. With a single twist of her arms, she toppled him out of the airlock and then pulled Mexone inside.

"With a little luck they might think he fell," she whispered. "Now to find some place where we can hide before any more come along."

In front of them was a long, wide corridor evidently leading towards the front of the vessel but behind them was a closed door. Knowing that if there were any more of the enemy still on board, they would be in the control room, the Amazon twisted the handle of the door. It opened instantly revealing another short passage.

"In here," she said urgently. "This seems to be the only place."

Three more doors led off the passage, each of them closed. The first was locked and the Amazon did not wish to burn through the lock with her welder. The Vorans might believe the guard had somehow lost his footing at the top of the ladder and fallen to his death but a smashed lock would instantly give away their presence on the spacecraft.

She tried the second door. It resisted for a moment as if the hinges were rusted and needed oiling. Then it swung open. It was evidently a storeroom piled high with metal and wooden boxes. There was a small oval porthole in the outer wall.

The Amazon forced a smile. "Judging by the state of those hinges, I'd say this room is hardly ever used." She pointed towards the far corner. "Let's make ourselves as comfortable as we can behind those boxes."

Even though they were empty, the boxes were extremely heavy but the Amazon lifted them as if they were made of paper, stacking them carefully, one on top of the other, leaving a space behind them sufficiently large for the three of them to sit.

"Now we just wait and see where this spaceship takes us." she said as they settled themselves. In spite of the fact that they had succeeded in getting aboard the enemy spaceship without being seen, there was still a worried frown on the Amazon's face.

Noticing it, Mexone said in a low voice, "You're still worried that we're walking blindly into a trap, aren't you, Amazon?"

To his surprise, she shook her head emphatically. "That isn't what worries me, Mexone. I just can't understand why that interdimensional wormhole brought us back to exactly the same place. It goes against everything I know about them. According to scientific theory, we should have found ourselves hundreds, or even thousands, of light years from that double-star system, much closer to the center of the galaxy. Yet if I'm to believe the evidence of my eyes, Uxxar is right back in orbit around that seetee sun. It's utterly senseless."

"Certainly it's beyond all reason the Vorans would simply return those natives to Thoron," Mexone admitted.

Before he could say anything more, the sound of harsh voices, muffled by the two intervening metal doors, reached them. The Amazon guessed immediately what was happening. The natives taken from Thoron were being brought on board. Heavy footsteps sounded in the near distance but no one came to the door through which they had come at the top of the airlock and they guessed the prisoners were being herded into some area closer to the nose of the spaceship.

The transport of the natives onto the vessel took the best part of half an hour. Then there came the loud metallic sound of the airlock being closed. A little while later the roar of the main engines vibrated through the ship.

"We're lifting off," Mexone said. "There's no going back now."

Acceleration pushed them against the floor of the small room. Once she judged they were clear of Uxxar's atmosphere and out in space, the Amazon eased herself to her feet and edged towards the oval port, steadying herself against the hull.

"What are you looking for?" Mexone asked softly. "There's nothing out there but stars."

"Stars—yes." The Amazon replied. "I'd hoped to see thousands of them but at the moment there's nothing but a black emptiness. We're still on the rim of the galaxy and no closer to an explanation of why we should find ourselves back where we began, unless—no, that's impossible."

"What is?"

The Amazon remained silent for so long that Mexone thought she had not heard his question, or did not intend to answer him. Then she turned and there was a strange expression on her face as she motioned to him to join her at the port. Pointing towards the scene outside, she said, "Do you see that small patch of hazy light?"

Mexone peered over her shoulder and then nodded. "Of course I can see it. We all saw it when we first dropped out of hyperspace. It's the Andromeda Nebula over two million light years away."

The Amazon shook her head. "No it isn't, Mexone. That is our own galaxy. We're now on the outer rim of the Andromeda Nebula. That wormhole transported us two million light years across that intergalactic gulf in virtually no time at all!"

CHAPTER 6

THE RUINED WORLD

THE Ultra dropped out of hyperspace on the very edge of the distant solar system. At that distance, the sun was little more than a very bright star, a little whiter than Sol with its surface temperature of around seven thousand degrees. Abna gradually reduced their speed to the point where the huge spaceship was hanging almost motionless in space.

His plan, which had earlier been agreed with Viona and Thania, was to examine each planet in turn as they moved closer to the parent sun. It was doubtful if any of the outer planets could have ever supported life of any kind with temperatures more than a two hundred degrees below zero. However, he did not mean to overlook the possibility that if a race had originated somewhere in this system, they might have discovered the secret of interplanetary flight. If so, it was conceivable they may have colonized all of the worlds around this star just as Earth had done hundreds of years earlier.

The outermost planet swam slowly into view on the screen. As expected, it was an ice world, its surface covered with frozen methane and other gases. It had no moon circling it like Pluto but as it passed slowly beneath them, they noticed something highly peculiar.

It was Viona who pointed it out to them. "What do you think that can be?" she asked.

The object in question was a vast metal pillar that towered over the planetary surface for almost two thousand feet. It pointed directly away from the distant sun towards the black empty space surrounding this system.

"Obviously it's artificial," Abna replied, frowning. "Since it's been erected here on the outermost world my guess would be that it's some kind of detection apparatus coupled to a powerful transmitter."

"Then it could be a distant warning system," Thania put in. "Put there to send a signal to someone if anything should come from outer space."

"Thania's right." Viona nodded. "If there is an intelligent race on one of these worlds, they put it here to give themselves a chance to defend their home world if they were attacked."

"So for some reason these people were afraid of an attack from outer space," Abna mused thoughtfully, turning the idea over in his mind.

"It could be the Vorans they are afraid of," Thania said. It was the first thought that came into her mind.

"That's possible, I suppose. After all, this system is only about ten light years from Thoron. Not long in hyperspace. If they are the invaders as we suspect, they could have visited most of the suns enclosed inside that barrier."

For several minutes they watched the lonely frozen world as it drifted away in its orbit. Then Abna applied more power to the engines and they proceeded sunward, towards the distant sun.

The next two planets they encountered were both large worlds very similar to Neptune and Uranus. The first had five moons of various sizes circling it and the second possessed a retinue of eight satellites, one of which was almost as large as Earth and clearly possessed an atmosphere of some kind. Unlike the other moons they had seen, all of which had cratered surfaces, this one appeared different.

Abna turned the Ultra slightly, saying, "I think we'll taker a closer look at this one. Even this far from the sun, it might have supported a colony." Inwardly, he was recalling how his ancestors had fled from Atlantis, finding a home on the surface of Jupiter, surviving under the most difficult conditions imaginable.

The instruments on the Ultra indicated that the atmosphere of this moon was composed almost entirely of hydrogen and methane.

"Are we going to land here?" Thania asked. For her, every new world was an adventure, filling her active mind with so many things she could scarcely imagine.

Abna shook his head. "I think we'll find that it's just another dead world. But there's something I want to check before we leave."

He increased the magnification slightly until the moon filled the entire screen. Clouds of methane crystals scudded across the surface driven by hurricane-force winds. Then he saw what he was looking for.

"There!" He pointed to the gap in the cloud cover. "Do you see them?"

The two girls peered over his shoulder. "You mean those odd domelike structures?" Thania asked.

"That's right. Those have been built some time in the past for use by either colonists or scientific expeditions. Now, as you can see, they're nothing more than smashed shells."

Viona remarked, "It doesn't look to me as though they've simply been abandoned and left to fall into ruins. They seem to have been deliberately destroyed."

"Exactly." There was a grim note to Abna's voice. "I think we'll find the same situation on all of the other planets and moons."

"You mean an entire race has been literally wiped out?" Viona leaned forward and peered more closely at the screen. "But who would do such a thing?"

Abna smiled but there was no mirth in the twitch of his lips. "Can't you guess?"

Thania stared at him. "You're really sure now it was the Vorans, that same reptilian species which is taking the Thorons for slaves?"

"At the moment, I'm absolutely certain and all of the evidence points the same way. That double-sun system is right on the doorstep of this one. That curious detector on the outermost planet was obviously designed as an early warning system against invaders from outer space." Sighing, he added, "We'll continue with our investigation of these planets but I'm betting we won't find a single survivor."

Moving sunward, they checked each planet and system of moons. Three huge gas planets occupied the central region of the planetary orbits, all attended by several satellites. On five of these they found evidence that colonies had been established, all beneath protective domes. In every case, the domes had been shattered as if some truly gigantic creature had stamped on them, splintering the tough material of which they were constructed.

Then, approximately a hundred million miles from the sun, they found the planet which had clearly spawned the intelligent race which had once dominated this solar system. It was a world that was so like the Earth that it could have been its twin.

Several continents and seas were visible beneath the cloud layer—but there the resemblance to Earth ended. Almost all of the land mass was covered with a blue-purple haze which, even from space, looked ominous and deadly. Violent storms rent the atmosphere in several places. Vivid lightning bolts laced the whirling clouds.

"What can that be?" Thania shivered slightly at the sight. "I've never seen anything like that before."

"No," Abna spoke through tightly-clenched teeth, "and it's something I hope you'll never see again. Only nuclear bombs could have caused all of that destruction. The entire civilization utterly wiped out by atomic explosions and hard radiation. I suppose it's possible that devastation was caused by a nuclear war between two opposing factions of that race. It almost happened on Earth before space travel was discovered."

Viona swiftly averted her gaze from the scene. "But you think it was the Vorans who did this?"

"There's only one way to find out. Go down there and take a look for ourselves."

"But you can't take the Ultra down there into all of that radiation," Thania protested, her eyes wide at the prospect.

Abna turned to face her. "You don't have to worry, Thania. No radiation can penetrate the hull of this spaceship. As for ourselves, we have special suits on board which will protect us from the radiation. I think we should leave Dorem here. He won't understand any of this."

"Is it wise to leave him on board alone?" Viona asked the blunt question.

"I'll stay with him if you like," Thania volunteered. Inwardly, she didn't like the look of the planetary surface and knew she would feel safer remaining where she was. Having now been given the super-strength of the Cmsaders, she knew she could handle the native without any trouble.

"Very well, Thania. You stay behind with Dorem. He now understands a little English, and once I lock the engine controls, there's no chance of him inadvertently doing any damage."

Before they put on the special suits, each of the Crusaders strapped a tiny instrument across one shoulder. "We must all wear this under our suits," Abna explained. "It's a miniature radiation monitor. In the unlikely event that any dangerous radiation penetrates the suit, this will give warning and we get back to the Ultra as quickly as possible."

The Ultra landed in the middle of a wide area close to what had once been a fair-sized town. As the huge spaceship touched down, the exhaust blasted away most of the rubble that littered the ground beneath it. Climbing down the ladder proved more difficult than usual since the protective suits were more cumbersome than those they normally used.

At the bottom, they paused in a small group and surveyed the scene around them.

Gaunt ruins clawed at the purple-tinged clouds overhead. Once there had been magnificent buildings here, wide paced streets and intersections. Now there was nothing but total ruin. Stone and metal had been vaporized when the bombs had rained down. Anyone caught in the open, or even indoors, would have been killed instantly.

Only those who happened to be deep underground might have escaped but Abna's rational, logical mind told him there would not have been many of them. After a while, even they would have perished from hunger and thirst, unable to return to the surface.

In the distance one of the thunderstorms they had witnessed earlier was passing across the horizon but a quick glance told them it was fortunately moving away from them.

Viona's voice came over the suit radios. "How long ago do you think this happened?"

Without turning his head, Abna replied, "Not too long. Judging by the intensity of the radiation and some of those atomic fires we saw, I'd say months rather than years."

"Then it's possible there may be some survivors?" she suggested.

Pausing a few yards in front of her Abna said, "That's highly unlikely. Maybe there are a few deep underground but we'd never find them."

Turning a corner where a once-proud building had stood—now nothing more than a mass of semi-molten rubble—they came upon a wide avenue. Like all of the others it was strewn with debris. Here and there, a few bodies were visible, all charred beyond recognition.

"This is terrible," Viona said with a catch in her voice. "All this wanton destruction—and for what? It isn't as if whoever did this needed these planets to live on—or even to defend themselves from these people."

"Unfortunately there are such evil races in the universe," Abna told her. "That is why we became the Cosmic Crusaders, to help prevent these atrocities being carried out on peaceful worlds. We've often found that such warlike civilizations are much stronger than their victims."

They paused halfway along the avenue where a low building seemed to have escaped much of the damage caused to the others. Abna motioned towards it, indicating they were to check inside. Entering it, they found themselves in a long room. The thick walls were lined with broad sheets of some kind of dense metal that seemed to have absorbed the shock of the bombs to a large extent.

"This might be a shelter of some kind," Viona observed, taking in every detail. "That would explain the way these walls have been constructed. They could also have absorbed much of the radiation."

There was very little in the way of furnishing in the room, merely low benches along the walls. In the far corner, however, was a closed door. Going over to it, Abna twisted the knob and pulled. For a moment, it resisted his efforts. Then, exerting all of his strength, he tugged it open.

A flight of stone steps led downward into utter darkness. Just inside the doorway, however, was a small switch. Reaching up, Abna flicked it on, not expecting anything to happen—if these people depended upon electricity, every generating station would certainly have been destroyed.

To his surprise light appeared along the length of the stairway. It came from small square sections in the right-hand wall, a pale luminous glow that seemed to be produced by some kind of chemical, rather than electrical, process.

"At least something still seems to be working despite all of this destruction," Viona said. "But just where does this stairway go?"

"We'll soon find out," Abna said.

Slowly, they descended the shaft, one behind the other. The steps seemed to go down forever, deep into the ground below the building. Then, when it seemed there was no end to them, they came up against a solid door. It looked thick and stout with broad metal bands across it.

Unlike the one at the top of the stairs, there appeared to be no visible means of opening it. Puzzled, Abna scrutinized its exterior. "It looks like a vault of some kind," he said after a brief pause.

"So what do we do now?" Viona inquired.

"We get in somehow." Abna took the small welding unit from his belt and a moment later, a spear of white-hot flame shot from the end. Swiftly, he applied the flame to the metal surface of the door. Within moments, molten drops hissed and fell to the floor but it was difficult work. Whatever the door was made of, the metal was extremely tough. Even the temperature of the mini-acetylene cutter was only just sufficient to melt it.

Working his way across the top of the door, Abna gradually cut through it; then set to down the sides. Sparks flew past his shoulders and Viona had to move back up the steps to avoid being hit by them.

Fifteen minutes later, however, Abna had cut a large rectangle in the metal. Shutting off the welder, he steps back a pace and then kicked out, putting all of his strength into his leg. The metal section fell inward and there was now a space large enough for them to squeeze through. Only darkness lay beyond the door. Here there were none of the phosphorescent plates that were spaced out down the wall of the shaft.

Fortunately, Abna had brought a small hand torch with him and clicking it on he shone the brilliant beam around the room. It was larger than he had expected but appeared to be completely empty. Then the beam fell on something in one corner.

At first, he thought it was nothing more than a bundle of discarded rags—but then it moved!

"What is it?" Viona's voice crackled eerily over the radio.

Abna went down on one knee, motioning her forward. "One of the inhabitants of this world," he answered. "And he seems to be still alive—but only just."

Reaching down, he drew the cloth covering the man's face aside. Wide, frightened eyes stared up at them from a white-haired, bearded face. A wrinkled hand went across the man's eyes as he tried to shield them from the bright torchlight.

"He must have come down here in an attempt to escape the destruction on the surface," Abna murmured softly. "Poor devil. Even that doesn't seem to have saved him. The radiation must have got to him before he could get inside for shelter."

The man's lips moved but for several moments nothing came out. Then in a halting voice, he said, "You are not...not those who came to destroy us."

The two Crusaders stared at him in stunned surprise. Finally, Viona found her voice. "He's speaking English," she said in amazement. "But how can that be?"

What might have passed for a faint smile twitched the man's lips. "We Oronians are skilled telepaths. I merely entered your minds and absorbed your language. It was not difficult."

Recovering from his astonishment, Abna said, "No, we did not come here with any warlike intentions. We are merely space explorers but we seem to have found ourselves in the middle of trouble. Do you know who did this to your planet?"

With an effort, the man nodded. "We first learned of their presence in this region of space when our ultra-telescopes picked up their vessels outside of our solar system. Our scientists quickly developed a means of detecting them if they approached our system of worlds. We have never developed space travel beyond our own planets, wishing only to live in peace and unmolested by any of our neighbors."

"So that is why you set up that large tower on your outermost planet?"

"Yes. We hoped it would give us sufficient time in which to devise ways of protecting ourselves if they should decide to attack. But their spaceships were too fast. They reached Oronia even before the warning signal from Karan, our outermost world, arrived."

The man swallowed thickly and his head sank back onto the floor. He lay so still that, for a moment, the Crusaders thought he was dead. After a few moments, however, he stirred himself again and levered himself up onto his elbows.

"You must not stay here. You can do nothing for me and even though they believed they have destroyed everyone on Oronia, they may return. They are fiends, creatures without any compassion or mercy. All they believe in is death and destruction."

"We think we've already encountered them," Abna said harshly. "Have you seen any of them?"

The man gave a weak shake of his head. "Not them—but we glimpsed their spaceship before the bombs began to rain down on us. They are not like the spacecraft we use for traveling to and from the planets and moons of our own worlds. They are monstrous vessels, all angles and bristling with weapons."

Abna nodded slowly. "I was right. The Vorans."

"Then you will know the kind of creatures they are—beings filled with evil and the lust for killing."

"Is there nothing you can do for him, Abna?" Viona seemed shocked by all that had happened.

"Very little, I'm afraid. He's already absorbed a highly lethal dose of hard radiation. Saving him is beyond even my powers. All I can do is to free him from pain…"

Taking the man's hand, Abna looked into his tortured eyes, and concentrated.

After a few moments, Abna's metaphysical efforts had a result. The man smiled and lifted a hand as if to acknowledge what Abna had done.

"Thank you, my friend. Go now. I have only a little time left before I join all of the others who have perished at the hands of these monsters."

Viona carefully placed the man's robe around him. There was an expression of shocked fury in her eyes as she stared at Abna. "I never thought I would agree with my mother about killing entire races," she said through her teeth, "but after what I've seen here I believe the Vorans should be utterly exterminated."

Abna got to his feet. "I can understand your feelings, Viona. In this case, those are exactly my sentiments. Knowing your mother, I think she'll be doing her best to do just that."

Before leaving, Abna turned back to the dying man in the corner. "Just one more question before we go. We need copper for our atomic engines. Do you know if any exists on any of your worlds?"

There was a long pause before the other answered. Then in a voice that was growing weaker by the minute, he said, "There is none on this world. That I do know. But—yes, I remember now. The only place you will find that chemical element is on Druuva, the small world nearest to our sun. Many years ago there was a mining expedition sent to that world. But that was long ago and the operation was abandoned."

After a respectful farewell to the dying man, they left the room and climbed the steps to the surface, going back out into the blasted ruins of the town.

CHAPTER 7

JOURNEY TO VORAN

IN the small storeroom on board the enemy vessel, the Amazon had recovered somewhat from her initial surprise at what had happened. Incredible as it seemed, she was forced to accept that this unique stellar system was completely identical with that situated on the rim of their own galaxy, even though the odds against it happening were billions to one.

Mexone, however, was still dubious. He did not have the mathematical skills of Abna and the Amazon but commonsense insisted that it was impossible. No matter how he tried to figure it out, it still went beyond all reason.

"How can two identical systems exist, hundred of millions of light years apart, each of them on the outer rims of two different galaxies?" He spoke so softly that the Amazon thought he was talking to himself. "Is it possible that space warp transported both suns and all three planets through this ultra-dimensional wormhole?"

"I'd like to believe that, Mexone," the Amazon replied. "Certainly it would make more sense—but that isn't the answer. Everything in that other system remained exactly where it was. We know that—because we saw it for ourselves. Only Uxxar vanished, nothing else."

Mexone shook his head. "Then all of this is beyond me, Amazon. I've seen a lot of strange things in the galaxy since I joined the Crusaders but nothing like this."

The Amazon stretched her legs to their full length to ease the cramp in her muscles. The vessel they were in was still accelerating at a tremendous rate.

Softly, the Amazon said, "Come to think of it, in an almost infinite universe, I suppose it would be impossible for something *not* to be duplicated. We'll just have to accept things as they are, Mexone, and—"

She broke off as she was suddenly gripped by a tremendous sense of strain. "I think— I think we're entering hyperspace," she gasped. "Brace yourself, Algar…"

Both The Amazon and Mexone experienced the—to them familiar—brief anguish as if they were being turned inside out. Algar groaned in terror. Then abruptly the feeling passed. The Thoron let out a shuddering sigh of relief.

"You were right, Amazon," Mexone said dryly, nodding towards the port. "Look over there."

Outside the port was the writhing gray mist of non-space. The Amazon looked once, then jerked her gaze away. She gripped the arm of Algar, who was staring, fascinated. "Look away now, Algar," she said firmly. "Prolonged staring at the enigma that is hyperspace can cause severe retinal and mental damage."

The Amazon turned to Mexone. "This seems to confirm that the Vorans come from another solar system. Let's hope it's not too distant…" she looked at her chronometer. We'll need to return to Uxxar before its next transit to our galaxy."

* * * *

It was several hours later when the trio were again gripped by a brief nausea and disorientation that presaged their vessel's re-emergence into normal space.

"It would seem we're coming to the end of this journey," the Amazon commented. "Now to see where we are and what kind of world this is."

Getting to her feet, she peered through the port. There was now the blackness of empty space all around them but a few moments later, the glaring disc of a red sun came into view as the spaceship turned. It was now spearing down towards a planet almost twice the size of Earth. As far as she could judge, it also seemed to be the only world orbiting this large sun.

She sat down again, placing her hands against the floor to brace herself as the spaceship began decelerating. Beside her, Algar murmured, "This is the world where these creatures take my people?"

The Amazon wasn't sure whether it was a statement or a question but it sounded like the former. However, she said, "This has to be that world, Algar. At the moment, any plans we make must be tentative. We've no idea what we're heading into. If we can discover where they keep your people and free them, we may have a chance. If not—well we won't think about that at the moment."

Mexone shrugged. "Quite honestly, Amazon, I can't see what the three of us can achieve against an entire planet—unless these creatures are more stupid than they seem and don't have guards anywhere."

The Amazon gave a grim smile. "I wouldn't rely on them being stupid, Mexone. They're clearly a highly intelligent race despite having evolved from reptiles. The main problem is that, apart from Algar, you and I will stand out like sore thumbs among the population. I'm relying on finding a place to hide before we're seen. I doubt if anyone will come here once we land so we wait until everyone leaves the spaceship."

She tried to shake off the feeling of helplessness that had now taken over her thoughts. This was not like her. Although she did not have Abna's calm and detached outlook, his ability to scan a problem and then find a logical solution, she was normally able to think clearly and coherently. In this situation, however, there were so many intangibles, so many things that could go wrong, that she could not see a clear way through them.

Better wait until we land and then see how things go, she told herself fiercely.

A little while later there came the thin scream of the atmosphere flowing past the sides of the vessel. Dark clouds appeared at intervals to obscure the swollen disc of the sun. Then there came a sudden jolt and a few seconds later silence returned as the note of the engines died away.

Taking care not to show herself to anyone watching outside, she peered around the side of the port. From their height above the ground she had a clear view of their surroundings. The landing ground was large and apart from a squat rectangular shed, was clearly situated some distance from the nearest buildings. About a mile away, the landscape was filled with ugly towers and squat domelike structures. All seemed to have been built with black stone with the exception of three high metal towers that shone reddish in the sunlight.

The architecture of the buildings was stark and bleak. Nowhere were there any graceful curves. Everything seemed to be composed of harsh angles and straight lines.

All in all it was a depressing scene that did nothing to lift her spirits.

The clang of the airlock being opened jerked her away from the port. Faintly, the three stowaways heard the rattle of the ladder dropping down the side of the hull. Crouching down behind the boxes, they waited tensely, ready to use their protonic blasters if anyone appeared. But no one came.

As they had suspected from the rusted state of the door hinges, this small section of the large vessel was very seldom used. At the moment, the Vorans would be busily engaged in transporting their prisoners through the airlock.

Risking another quick look through the port, the Amazon saw that the natives were now shackled together with heavy chains around their ankles. They were being herded across the landing field with several Voran guards on either side of them. She felt her teeth clench as she saw the way they were being treated, more like animals than human beings.

The sight made her more determined than ever to free as many of them as possible and return them to their home planet. At the moment, however, that was easier said than done.

An hour passed. Then she heard the unmistakable sound of the airlock being closed.

Mexone had also heard it. Smoothly, he got to his feet, making no noise.

"You think they've all gone, Amazon?" he asked in a low voice.

"I think so. Now they've landed on their home world they won't need anyone left on board. I'd say they'll leave this craft here until the time comes to return to Uxxar and that won't be for several days yet."

The storeroom door creaked loudly as she forced it open and peered into the short corridor. When nothing happened, she motioned her companions outside. Not a sound disturbed the silence inside the spaceship.

Her weapon ready in her right hand, she opened the second door and stepped into the airlock. The long corridor leading to the front of the vessel was deserted. Algar stepped forward a couple of paces. After a moment, he said quietly, "There is no one here. They have all left."

Mexone stared at him in surprise. "How can you be so certain of that, Algar?"

What passed for a smile twisted the native's lips. "We live in that dense jungle on Thoron where there are many enemies. We can tell when there are any within our sensing range."

"Then if you're right, I want to take a look at the controls of this spaceship." Trusting to Algar's strange sense, she thrust the protonic gun back into its holster and commenced to walk along the corridor.

Mexone wasn't sure what the Amazon had in mind but he followed her without question. Several narrower lateral passages led off the main one but the Amazon ignored these, continuing straight ahead until finally they emerged into the large control room.

Some parts of it the Amazon recognized from that image she had seen on the screen when the Voran commander had threatened to destroy them. Long rows of tiny bulbs stretched in a semi-circle in front of the viewing screen. Levers and buttons covered the lowermost banks of the instrument panel. All of the bulbs were dead and she guessed that every system inside the craft had been switched off.

Eyeing them, Mexone said, "There's obviously no power going into these instruments now, Amazon. That means the air system has been shut down."

Without turning, the Amazon said confidently. "There's still plenty of air inside the ship to last us for as long as I intend to stay."

Without saying anything more, she allowed her keen glance to pass over the intricate array of controls. The entire layout was similar to that on board the Ultra although the curious symbols meant nothing to her.

After a few minutes of silence, Mexone asked, "Why the sudden interest in these, Amazon? You're not going to try to steal this ship, are you?"

"Not at the moment but if everything works out—and that's a big if, I know—we'll need some means of escaping from this planet and getting back to Uxxar before it disappears again."

Once she was satisfied, she pointed to the viewing screen; then turned to face her companions. "I suggest we remain here until it is dark. Judging by the position of the sun I'd say that won't be more than a couple of hours. From the rate it has moved across the sky since we landed, I believe this planet revolves on its axis somewhat faster than Earth."

* * * *

Slowly, the carmine glow outside faded as the giant sun dipped towards the horizon. The last red rays touched the ugly buildings with a lurid red glow. Not daring to use any form of illumination, the trio moved to the airlock in complete darkness. Throughout the time they had kept a close watch there had been very little activity around the three spaceships that had traveled from Uxxar. Even around the perimeter there was no sign of any guards.

Evidently the Vorans were supremely confident that no one would approach the vessels once their hostages had been taken away. However, this apparent lack of any security both pleased and worried the Amazon. It might make the task of getting out of this vessel without being seen easier. It could also mean that the Thoron captives were so securely locked away somewhere that it was virtually impossible for them to escape.

"Are we all ready?" she asked with her hand on the airlock handle.

"Ready," Mexone nodded. Algar looked doubtful but said nothing.

With a smooth movement, the Amazon turned the handle, thrusting the heavy door open with ease. A blast of hot air brushed their faces; a wind filled with strong, but unrecognizable odors.

Glancing down, the Amazon saw that the extendable ladder was still in place against the hull. Was this another lack of security? Possibly the idea that anyone would dare to interfere with these vessels was alien to their reptilian minds.

They made a swift descent. The only sound that disturbed the stillness was a continuous harsh droning noise that came from the direction of the nearby city. It grated on their nerves as they ran, doubled over, for the metal fence.

Reaching it, they crouched down while the Amazon took the small portable welder from her belt and ignited the white-hot flame.

"Let us hope there are no sharp eyes watching," she muttered as she began slicing through the tough metal.

Within a few minutes she had cut away a large square section of the barrier, big enough for them to crawl through. Straightening up on the other side, they scanned the area around them. The nearest buildings were about a quarter of a mile away, gaunt square shapes with ugly abutments attached to the walls.

Clearly this was a city that bespoke great technical and scientific achievement but none of it seemed to be devoted to peaceful pursuits. Every harsh line and contour indicated a race totally dedicated to war and domination, the enslavement of entire worlds. It was a cruel and hard world that had bred a race of cruel people—if the term could be applied to such reptilian monsters.

Somehow, running as fast as possible, they reached the nearest building without being seen. The streets were narrow, crossed at irregular intervals by metal walkways. Here, the droning, throbbing noise they had heard earlier was louder, hammering stridently at their ears.

The Amazon glanced in Mexone's direction. "That sounds like heavy machinery, and I don't have to guess what it is they're manufacturing."

"Weapons and more spaceships." Mexone gave an almost imperceptible nod. "1 shudder to visualize what would happen if a massive fleet was assembled and they decided to launch a surprise attack on our galaxy."

The Amazon turned the thought over in her mind. It was one that appalled her—and from what she knew of this race, it was something that could happen unless she could somehow prevent it.

Hundreds, perhaps thousands, of civilization could be annihilated if the Vorans should decide to extend their belligerent campaign beyond that small region of space they had already invaded. This would be warfare on a galactic scale and it was difficult to tell which side would win. Whatever the outcome, entire worlds in the galaxy could be consumed in atomic fire.

Resting his shoulders against the wall, Mexone said suddenly, "You seem awfully quiet and preoccupied, Amazon. Something on your mind?"

The Amazon gave a mental shrug. "Sorry. I was just considering what would happen if a whole fleet of Voran spaceships was to land on Uxxar, be transported back to our galaxy, ready to launch a full-scale attack."

"You think that's possible?"

"Why not? I'll wager that virtually all of these buildings are producing armaments and if this is being repeated all over this planet, it won't be long before they're ready."

"So this is why my people are being brought here," Algar said bitterly. "To produce weapons of destruction."

"I'm afraid so, Algar," the Amazon affirmed. "I can't think of any other reason. The Vorans think nothing of killing any races who threaten them. It's the only reason they allow you to live instead of wiping you out."

Algar's features hardened into a mask of determination. He said grimly, "Then I am glad you brought me with you. I will do anything you ask if it will free my people and stop this war you speak of."

For a moment, the Amazon was on the point of assuring him that he was an essential part of her plan but instead, she said briskly, "But this isn't the time to talk about this. Right now, we have to find somewhere we can hide. They won't be looking for us but we have to keep out of sight until I can size up this situation."

Now that it was dark there were lights visible, placed at irregular intervals along the street. Fortunately they were dim and the shadows around the trio were large and deep. Keeping well in to the wall, they moved silently along the row of huge buildings, eyes and ears alert for any sound or movement.

Twenty yards along the street they came upon a narrow alley where there were no lights. One after the other, they moved into it, pausing to allow their eyes to adjust to the intense darkness. Gradually, they were able to make out vague details.

A high wall extended along either side. Most of the tall buildings were set close to it, overlooking the length of the alley but a short distance away was a smaller building, set well back from the wall. No lights showed in any of them.

The Amazon pointed towards the small structure, leading them to the wall that fronted it. "This looks the most likely place," she whispered. "You go up first, Mexone. We can't use the nylon cord, there's nothing up there to attach it to."

Stepping in front of him, she bent her knees slightly. Mexone paused for a moment and then placed his hands on her shoulders, pulling himself up until he was standing on them. Straightening her legs, the Amazon lifted him until his stretching fingers were hooked around the top of the wall. Gripping his ankles, she thrust him up until he was safely on top.

Turning to Algar she could just make out the look of amazement on his features. "It's your turn now, Algar," she said softly. "Up you go." Towering over her, the native hesitated. He seemed on the point of shaking his head. "Don't worry, Algar," she went on. "I've lifted far heavier weights than you."

Still dubious, Algar climbed onto her shoulders. The next moment she was holding him easily high over her head as his fingers scrabbled for the top of the wall. Mexone helped him onto it and then leaned down to catch the Amazon by the wrist. Smoothly, he drew her up until she was beside them.

Together, they dropped down onto the ground on the other side. The wide door in the wall was securely locked but that proved no hindrance to Mexone. His welder sliced through the metal of the lock as if through butter. A few moments later they were all inside, the door closed behind them.

Taking out her small torch, the Amazon shone the beam around the large room. There were shelves along three of the walls and examining the contents of the boxes on them, the Amazon said. "This seems to be a food store. At least we won't go hungry during our stay here."

"If this food is edible," Mexone cautioned. "What might be good for reptiles may not necessarily be good for humans."

The Amazon checked her belt. Whenever there was the possibility of a prolonged stay on some new world, they always carried a supply of food pills in their pouches, small capsules which contained all of the vitamins and minerals necessary to sustain life.

After checking out the building, they made themselves as comfortable as possible on the floor behind what looked like a counter. It was unlikely anyone would come there during the night.

Yet even though she was tired, the Amazon was unable to sleep. The incessant noise from the city kept her awake, dinning in her ears. At times, it was so loud that she felt the building shudder around her. Finally, unable to content herself, she got to her feet, taking care not to disturb the others.

At the front of the store was a large window and she went over to it, looking out into the street that lay beyond. The absence of any of the Vorans still nagged at her. It was unlikely they were all asleep except for those obviously operating all of the machinery.

A sudden movement at the far end of the street caught her attention. Swiftly, she stepped back from the window, pressing her shoulders against the wall so that she could see without being seen. A group of about twenty Vorans came striding along the street. All of them were armed and appeared to be guards.

Watching intently, she saw them pause outside a tall building not far from the perimeter of the landing field. The leader unlocked the door and motioned the others inside. Several minutes passed and nothing else happened. Then two of the guards came out and stood, one on either side of the door, their weapons in their hands.

A long file of Thorons emerged. By the time the Voran leader relocked the door, the Amazon estimated there were close on fifty of the natives. This time, none of them were shackled. They stood submissively in the street, heads bowed, their arms hanging loosely at their sides, as the guards formed up on either side of them.

Uttering a loud command, the Voran in charge led them along the street, past the window where the Amazon stood watching. They had only gone fifty yards when one of the natives suddenly broke away from the others. Weaving from side to side, he ran for the opposite side of the street. Instantly, one of the guards raised his weapon.

A shaft of blue light flashed from the muzzle. The native threw up his arms as the bolt of energy struck him between the shoulders. There was a burst of brilliance that momentarily dazzled the Amazon. When she could see clearly again there was no sign of the Thoron. He had vanished as if the earth had swallowed him completely.

The Amazon had seen that kind of weapon before—a kind of atomic disintegrator. Pressing her lips tightly together, she forced herself to keep a close watch on the scene outside.

Moving the remaining captives on, the Vorans stopped before one of the large buildings. Half of the natives were ushered inside with two of the guards. Then the remainder was marched along the street, disappearing from sight around a corner.

The Amazon turned away from the window to find Mexone standing silently beside her. "Did you see anything of what happened out there?" she asked in a harsh whisper.

"I saw them slaughter that native who tried to escape," he replied with a brittle edge to his voice.

The Amazon pointed towards the tall building standing on the nearby corner. "They brought them from there. My guess is that they keep them locked inside that building and then take out as many as they need, working in shifts night and day, to operate all of the machines in this city."

CHAPTER 8

SOLAR DESTRUCTION

THE innermost planet of the Oronian system was, like Mercury in the Solar System, a world of extremes of temperature. Always turning the same hemisphere towards the sun, one side was a blistering hell with a temperature close to two thousand degrees Celsius. The other half, which never saw any sunlight, lay in perpetual darkness, facing the almost absolute zero conditions of outer space.

Scrutinizing it keenly on the visiscreen, Abna readily saw that it was exactly as that dying Oronian had described. It was a world impossible for anyone to live on for any length of time. Yet the Oronians had come here to mine for precious metals. Like the Earth's Moon, this planet's axis oscillated around a small circle instead of constantly maintaining the same alignment in space. As a result there was a very narrow twilight zone where the sun rose and set a little way above the bare horizon.

Here, the temperature was not ideal—but tolerable and here it was that the Oronians had set up their mining installations.

Watching the planet below them Viona asked, "Do you think we'll find any copper here, Dad?"

"I hope so. Our supply is running pretty low and if we don't find some soon we could be in trouble. If there is any, it will be quite a simple matter to purify it and shape into the cubes we need for the engines."

Glancing across the control room to where Thania stood deep in thought, he went on, "You seem to have something on your mind, Thania. What is it?"

The girl turned and walked over. "I suppose I'm worried about the Amazon. She could be in big trouble wherever that planet has taken her and there's absolutely nothing we can do to help. I've a lot to thank her for, making me a Crusader after my parents were murdered. I wouldn't want anything to happen to her. Nor to Mexone."

Abna nodded. "I understand how you feel, Thania. But Vi's well able to take care of herself. The only way we can help her now is to get enough copper and be back there for when Uxxar reappears. She's been in tighter spots than this and come through them. And Mexone's no slouch, either."

His words seemed to reassure her a little for she gave a smile. "Of course you're right. You've known her a lot longer than I have."

"I have," Abna agreed, "and I know just what she's capable of. She thrives on getting herself into dangerous situations just to help oppressed people. Now help me search for these mining settlements."

Slowly, the Ultra made a complete circuit of the small planet. Although they scanned the narrow strip of the twilight zone diligently, they saw no sign of anything but barren rock and large craters.

Disappointed, Abna said, "We'll go around again and use a higher magnification this time. There has to be something if that Oronian spoke the truth."

Easing the huge vessel into a lower orbit, they swung around the planet once more. At first, it seemed their second scan would be no more successful than the first. Then Thania's keen eyes spotted something on the floor of a massive crater that extended all the way across the zone.

Easing back on the power to the engines, Abna brought the Ultra to an almost complete stop. Leaning forward, he studied the crater floor intently; then gave a nod.

"I think you're right, Thania. There seems to be some kind of artificial structure down there. We'll go down and take a look."

Deftly, he manipulated the controls so that the Ultra landed gently on its tail, raising a cloud of dust that settled swiftly in the absence of any atmosphere. Once they had put on their suits and helmets, they climbed out of the airlock and down the ladder, leaving Darem on board. By now he had become accustomed to life on the huge vessel.

The crater floor was covered in a thick cloud of very fine dust. Overhead, the sky was almost black but there was a faint yellow glow along one horizon, outlining the crater wall in that direction. Through their transparent helmets they picked out the small cluster of buildings close against the crater rim.

Even from that distance they looked empty and abandoned. There was, however, very little evidence of decay.

Over the suit radios, Thania said, "It's hard to believe they've been here for any length of time. They look quite new as if they'd been erected only a few days ago."

"That's what we would expect," Abna explained. "There's no atmosphere here to cause any rusting and no wind to lift the dust and corrode any of the metal. They'll probably be like this in a thousand years time."

It was only as he said this that he realized something he should have noticed earlier. If men from Oronia had worked this mine there should have been a protective dome erected over the entire site. Even if the operators and miners had worn spacesuits while working, they could not have done so while eating and sleeping.

Viona noticed his puzzled expression. "Is there something wrong, Dad?" she asked.

"Something odd rather than wrong," he said. "There's a vacuum here, all over the site. How did they eat and sleep?"

They found the answer in one of the huts. As they entered it, Abna reached instinctively for the gun in his belt; then paused. What he had taken for a line of men standing motionless against the far wall were robots. Walking forward, with Viona and Thania following close behind him, he examined them closely. "These are clearly highly sophisticated creations," he said finally. "Robots equipped with electronic brains. They would do all of the manual labor—drilling for the ore, smelting and refining the metals they dug out of the crater—a wonderful achievement."

"Only for those who created them to be destroyed utterly by the Vorans." Thania put in bitterly.

A number of large drilling units stood around the huts. Eyeing them closely, Abna guessed that they had been used to drill deep through the crater floor. Metal rails ran from each of them towards a larger building and there were several large trucks in evidence, obviously used to carry the ore to the refinery.

Entering the nearest shed next to that housing the robot workers, they found a large number of mining items, what were clearly pickaxes and shovels, stacked neatly against one wall. In the center was a small table with scrolls lying on it. Most were covered with a strange script which none of them could decipher.

"Evidently these are records of some kind giving details of everything that has been mined," Viona observed. "But there doesn't seem to be anything else of interest."

"I suggest we take a look in that large shed," Abna said. "It seems to be where all of the ore was taken."

They trudged through the ankle deep dust to the perimeter of the site, stepping carefully over the metal rails. Here there was a large opening to permit the entry and exit of the big ore trucks. Easing his way around one that almost completely blocked the entrance, Abna flashed the beam, of his torch around him. The powerful light showed massive cauldrons obviously used for smelting.

Pointing to then, he said, "Whatever method they used for refining the ores, it couldn't have been electricity for there's no sign of any generators. They were possibly sufficiently advanced to use some form of nuclear heating."

They moved to the rear of the building. Here they found themselves in luck. Several large metal bins stood against the wall, nearly all of them filled with large metal ingots. After a quick check, Abna found the one he wanted.

"Copper," he said with a note of satisfaction in his voice. "We're in luck and I'd say this is one hundred percent pure. We'll take as many of these ingots as we can carry back to the Ultra. Then we'll—"

He broke off sharply as a sudden faint sound reached them from outside. It was the first sound they had heard since landing on the planet. Here, in this twilight zone, the virtual vacuum was alleviated by escaping internal gases—sufficient to have carried the sound.

Quickly, they ran to the opening, peering around them. At first they saw nothing to account for the noise. Then Viona glanced up at the sky and pointed. The light of the nearby sun glistened off something moving rapidly across the heavens like a shooting star.

"The Voran spaceship!" Abna spoke the words through his teeth. "They must have come searching for us once they realized we were no longer in that other planetary system. At the moment they're too far away to have seen the Ultra inside this deep crater."

"But they'll no doubt keep looking for us," Viona said with urgency and alarm in her voice.

Each of them carrying several of the ingots in their arms, the trio ran swiftly towards the spaceship. The impeding dust slowed their progress but at last they reached the ladder and clambered quickly on board. Closing the airlock, Abna deposited the copper at the side of the controls and then shrugged out of the spacesuit.

The enemy spacecraft was no longer visible having passed out of sight around the limb of the planet. From what he had seen it appeared that the enemy commander had been searching the night side of the world but sooner or later, he would turn his attention to the narrow twilight zone. They had to be clear of the planet before that happened. If the Vorans attacked while they were still on the surface they would have little chance of fighting back.

To Viona, he said urgently, "Take two of those copper ingots and use that machine over there to slice them into squares and then feed two of them into the power plant's matrix. I want every ounce of speed we can get out of the Ultra."

As Viona hurried to do as he said, Thania asked, "You've got a plan, Abna?"

"A plan yes—but I should warn you all that it's extremely dangerous and one which will require split second timing. The slightest error and we'll all be finished."

A few moments later, the atomic engines roared and the Ultra lifted smoothly from the crater and headed out into space. By then, Abna guessed the enemy ship was somewhere on the other side of the planet but knowing the enemy, he reckoned it would not be long before the Ultra was spotted.

Viona had been considering the same thing. Through tight lips, she said, "Are you hoping to escape without being seen?"

Abna shook his head. "On the contrary, I want to be seen. All I need is to stay well ahead of them until we reach Dorem's solar system."

Viona shook her copper-colored hair in obvious bewilderment. "But what good will that do us? Even there they're sure to hunt us down. There's no place there to hide."

Adjusting the controls, Abna set the viewing screen so that it projected the area of space directly behind them. The bright yellow sun was now dwindling swiftly as they fled into the endless dark.

Glancing at the screen, he said tautly, "There they are. Now they have us in sight they'll follow us wherever we go."

Perplexed, Thania said, "I still don't understand. Perhaps I don't know too much about space travel, but—"

Interrupting her, Abna said in a curiously calm tone, "I'm leading them into a trap, Thania, and we are the bait." There was an expression on Abna's face that she had not seen before—a grim, coldly calculating look that almost frightened her.

"What kind of trap?" It was Viona who spoke now. She was still standing by the power matrix, expertly slicing the second copper ingot into the correct-sized cubes.

"You'll see once we get there. Once I'm certain they've plotted our course and know where we're going, I'm taking the Ultra into hyperspace. Whatever happens, I don't want them to lose us."

"I still don't understand what you intend to do?" Thania kept her eyes on the screen. Now they were in empty space, she could no longer make out the enemy vessel—but she knew it was still there, clinging to their trail like a leech.

"Nor I," Viona said without turning her head. "But whatever it is, we'll both do exactly as you say, won't we Thania?"

"Of course." The other girl spoke without any hesitation.

"Good. You've just got to trust me." It went against the grain for him to take this life-or-death decision without consulting them but he knew that if he told them what he had in mind it would almost certainly frighten them out of their wits and they would try to dissuade him from the only course that lay open to them if the Vorans were to be destroyed.

Swiftly, the Ultra approached the speed of light as he fed more and more power to the engines. Then there came a moment when thin scream of the engines was cut off and they were briefly gripped by strain and nausea. They had entered hyperspace. Swiftly, Abna closed the shutter across the viewing screen so that they were unable to see outside. Non-space was not something human eyes could look at for long without going insane.

* * * *

Since time had no meaning in hyperspace it was impossible for the Crusaders to estimate how long they spent in that strange continuum. Most of the time they spent sleeping. When they emerged into normal space and Abna removed the shield from in front of the viewer, they saw that behind them, space was empty. The enemy vessel was almost certainly still in hyperspace.

Swinging the viewer, Abna focused it on the region into which they were heading, cutting their velocity slightly as he did so. The scene in front of them was frighteningly familiar. The two suns were clearly visible just over a billion miles away, moving in their endless orbits.

Resolutely, Abna said, "Now we're here, I'll tell you what I intend to do. We're all agreed that this Voran vessel has to be destroyed, together with all those creatures on board. I've gone over every possibility in my mind but there's only one chance and as I said earlier, it puts us all in a lot of danger."

Stoutly, Viona declared, "If we were afraid of dying every time we came across a situation like this, we wouldn't be worthy of the name—The Cosmic Crusaders."

"I'm glad you feel that way—because my plan is to lead that Voran spaceship directly into that seetee sun! Playing tag with a solar furnace is a classic maneuver that was first carried out by the Golden Amazon herself to destroy an alien armada." He smiled reminiscently. "That was before you were born, Viona. The consequences of it led directly to my meeting your mother."

"Into the sun?" There was disbelief in Thania's voice. "But that would be suicidal. Even the Ultra can't withstand that." She glanced round at Viona standing open-mouthed at the end of the control panel. "Can it?"

Viona shook her head emphatically. "No—it can't. Mother once told me of her exploit, but she was dealing with an ordinary sun. This sun is made of antimatter! Once we come into contact with that, the ship and everything in it, including ourselves, will go up in a blaze of radiation. Within a microsecond, we'll all be annihilated."

She stared almost pleadingly at Abna. "Surely you're not serious?"

"I'm being perfectly serious," he replied gravely. "I realize that the closer we approach that sun, the more intense the antimatter radiation will be in the form of the solar wind. But I can plot a course that will skim just above the outer surface of that sun and if we're traveling at a fraction less than the speed of light, we'll be in and out of there within half a minute."

"But what damage will that do to the hull of the Ultra?" Viona asked. "Being bombarded with antimatter particles for even half a minute must cause some of the material to be destroyed."

"And have you taken the gravitational pull of that sun into account?" Thania inquired. She was trying not to show the fear in her mind at the idea of diving headlong towards that sun.

Abna remained in thoughtful silence for a while. Then he said, "I intend to take everything into consideration when I plot our course. But a lot will depend upon the two of you. I can work out our trajectory and our velocity—as well as fly the Ultra. Viona, you must stand by the power matrix and be ready to feed in more copper if it's needed."

"And what do you want me to do, Abna?" Thania asked.

"I need you to keep a close watch on the enemy vessel, let me know exactly what it is doing. A lot is going to depend on it following us closely, so close that when I make a sudden turn there'll be no time for them to pull out of their course—straight into that sun."

Reaching forward, he depressed a small switch which had the effect of splitting the image on the viewing screen in half, enabling them to watch the scenes unfolding outside from both front and rear at the same time. Then he turned on his heel, leaving Thania to keep watch and walked quickly to the console to make his final calculations. He knew everything had to be exact, down to the last little detail. Yet even if he got everything correct, it was going to be touch and go—possibly the biggest gamble of his life.

A minute later a call from Thania brought his head up sharply. "The Voran vessel has dropped out of hyperspace, Abna. I can just make it out."

"How far is it behind us?" Abna snapped.

"It's still several million miles away but coming up fast."

"Good. I'm almost finished here."

Two minutes later, he was back at the main controls. Ahead of them the two suns almost filled the left-hand half of the screen. Smoothly, he adjusted a dial to reduce the intolerable glare as much as possible. In the other section the Voran spaceship was a small dot that rapidly grew larger as the enemy put on more speed in an attempt to catch up with them.

"Now we'll see if the Voran commander takes the bait," he said grimly. "Are the copper cubes all ready, Viona?"

"All ready to be loaded into the matrix when you give the word," she replied. Her voice was calm and controlled but Abna knew that inwardly she was just as tensed as they all were. Success or failure now rested on split-second timing and the absolute accuracy of his calculations.

Leaving Thania to keep watch on the approaching enemy vessel, he concentrated all of his attention on the solar system now almost directly ahead of them. Ignoring the giant blue sun completely, he stared at the innocent-looking yellow sun. He had deliberately plotted their course so that they were approaching along a path that would take them clear of the highly unstable zone between the two bodies. Whatever happened, he did not want to venture to close to that region of space.

"I'm increasing our velocity now," he said gravely. "This is not going to be pleasant for any of us. Just hang on and with luck we'll come through it in one piece."

Beside him, Thania said, "The Vorans have put on more speed. It looks as though they intend to follow us all the way."

"That's what I'm hoping for. All we have to do now if stay ahead of them until the last moment." On the left-hand side of the screen the glare was now almost blinding. The surface of the seetee sun now filled it entirely. Huge prominences leapt high into its chromosphere. Vast sunspots showed as ragged-edged areas of a slightly lower temperature than the rest.

Vortices of spiraling energy twisted close to the bases of the prominences. Inside the cabin the temperature began to rise swiftly even though the refrigeration systems within the Ultra were working at full power.

Fighting against the acceleration, the three of them stood ready. Perspiration dripped into their eyes as the heat continued to mount. Above the shrill roar of the engines, a faint crackling sound now became audible.

"What can that noise be?" Thania asked tensely. "It seems to be coming from somewhere outside the Ultra."

"We're being bombarded by antimatter particles," Abna told her. "Wherever they strike the hull they annihilate a particle of the metal.

Fortunately the hull is thick but there's no doubt they would shatter it completely if we were to stay in this area long enough. If my plan works that will happen to that enemy spaceship. Are they still close on our tail?"

"Yes. They can't be more than five hundred miles away now. Why don't they use their weapons?"

"Who knows what those creatures are thinking? There's no doubt they intend to finish us this time. Perhaps they're hoping the gravitational pull of this sun will do that job for them."

Now he divided his attention between the two images on the screen. Already, the Voran ship was les than three hundred miles away and closing swiftly. A quick glance at the velocimeter told him they were now traveling at ninety percent light velocity.

Judging by how quickly the Voran craft was closing the gap between them he estimated that the enemy commander was also pushing his engines to their limit.

"Hold on everyone," he called. As he pushed forward the lever in front of him, he said, "Feed two of those copper cubes into the power matrix, Viona."

The girl obeyed instantly and then clutched hard at the supports as Abna hauled on the elevation lever. Shuddering throughout its entire length, the Ultra altered course, the nose pointing away from the sun towards the blackness of space.

Terrific pressure threatened to pull them away from their holds. Desperately, they hung on, the superhuman muscles in their arms flexing to their limit. For an instant, blackness spun in front of Thania's vision. Then it passed and she could see clearly again.

On the visiscreen, Abna and Thania had a clear view of the Voran vessel. They saw it begin to spin as the commander realized too late that he was dropping straight into the raving chaos of the sun. As Abna had hoped, the Voran had been too filled with the desire to destroy them that he had not recognized his danger in time.

Unable to slow down, the ugly vessel fell towards the solar surface. There was a moment when it was visible as a black shape against the vicious glare. Then it vanished in a brilliant flash of annihilated atoms, so bright that the brief glow shone brighter than the fiery background of the sun's disc.

But the Ultra was not yet out of danger. The atomic engines shrilled and whined as they struggled to break free of the sun's gravity. On the velocimeter, the red needle edged slowly downward as their speed commenced to fall. Tight-lipped, Abna dashed the perspiration from his eyes and coaxed more power into the engines. Already, they were in danger of being overloaded.

Close to where Viona was standing fuses blew, only to be quickly replaced as she struggled to remain on her feet against the grueling pressure. The needle on the velocimeter stopped. Then slowly, painfully slowly, it commenced to rise again. At times, it seemed they were not going to make it—and all the while the stream of antiparticles from the solar surface was hammering against the outer hull.

Then they were moving more quickly with the raging furnace falling away behind them. Not until they were more than ten million miles from the sun did Abna slow the Ultra to cruising speed and force himself to relax. Inside the control room the temperature now fell swiftly.

"We did it!" Thania exclaimed excitedly. "We've totally destroyed that Voran vessel."

Abna nodded. "I think we should see how Dorem fared during the encounter with that sun. Then we'll head for Thoron and reunite him with his people."

The native was unconscious on the floor of the room where he had been left. He appeared to have suffered no injuries and soon came round as Thania tended to him.

Once he was sure that the native was all right, Abna said, "I'll set a course for Thoron and then impress a little English into his brain so that we can communicate with the others once we land. With all danger from the Vorans gone for the time being, Thoron will be the best place for us to remain until Uxxar returns to this system."

A little over an hour later, the Ultra landed smoothly on Thoron. Abna put the spaceship down in the same clearing as before just a short distance from the pinnace they had left. Once they had all descended to the ground, Abna and Viona moved slowly around the huge craft examining the exterior of the hull for damage caused by the impact of the antiparticles.

Here and there they spotted areas where the tough metal had been scored and pitted but surprisingly the damage appeared to be mainly superficial. Nodding his head in satisfaction, Abna led the small group towards the dense jungle. Before landing he had telepathically impressed a basic knowledge of English into Dorem's brain. Now he was able to converse freely with them.

They entered the tall trees with Dorem in the lead. This time the titan jungle denizens remained quiescent, evidently recognizing there was now no danger from them. Dorem led them along the narrow track for half a mile and then motioned to them to stop. Even though the wide clearing in front of them was empty, there was still the feel of being watched by hidden eyes.

Cupping his mouth with his hands, Dorem uttered a loud, piercing whistle and then commenced to call something in the strange clicking language. For several minutes nothing happened. Then there was movement among the surrounding trees. A large party of the natives appeared, advancing cautiously through the dense undergrowth. They all looked wary and suspicious but they carried their long spears by their sides and made no warlike move against the Crusaders.

Dorem walked towards the tallest native and spoke rapidly to him. After a short conversation, Dorem came back. There was a broad smile on his face. "Kardi is the—how do you say it—chief of our tribe. I have told him much of what has happened, that you are not enemies like the Vorans and also that you have destroyed their spaceship. He welcomes you in peace. Now there is no danger you may remain here with us until Algar and your friends return."

"Tell him that we thank him for allowing us to remain," Abna said.

Once Dorem had relayed the message to Kardi, the chief raised his spear and pointed towards the far side of the clearing, indicating that they were to follow him.

Flanked by the rest of the natives, they crossed the clearing, walked along another narrow trail, and then emerged into a large open space dotted with dozens of small huts.

Dorem led them to one of the huts. "You may rest here. I will see to it that food and drink are brought for you."

Entering the hut they found it was spacious with a number of low beds woven from large leaves spread out on the floor. Viona eyed them somewhat dubiously but flinging herself down on one of them, Thania exclaimed, "These are far more comfortable than they look."

While the two girls rested, Abna went outside and waited for Dorem to return. Taking the native on one side, he said, "Once we've eaten, I have some questions I would like to ask your chief. I'll need you to translate for me."

Dorem nodded. "I will tell him. If we can help you in any way should the Vorans come back, we will do so."

CHAPTER 9

CAPTURE

FOR the Amazon, the night passed slowly, each individual minute dragging itself out like an eternity. She did not sleep but maintained a constant watch on the street outside. The scene she had witnessed earlier was repeated several times through the hours of darkness. Occasionally, small groups of the natives were brought back from some place in the city and thrust into the huge building.

By the time the dawn broke she had a clear picture of what was happening on Voran. She did not doubt that these creatures were gearing up for all-out war. The throbbing drone of heavy machinery had continued without pause, vibrating through the still air until her head ached.

While she had kept her nocturnal vigil, she had considered a number of options. Most of them she had instantly dismissed as being either far too dangerous—or impossible.

Now there was only one plan in her mind.

As Mexone got up from behind the long counter, she put her plan to him. "From what I see, there's only one place safe from discovery. My guess is that soon, this entire city will be teeming with Vorans."

"I agree. So where do you suggest we go?"

The Amazon lifted a hand and pointed a finger directly upward. "Up there—onto the top of one of these buildings. I had a good look at that landing field before we left and one thing struck me as odd. There were several spaceships parked there but not a single smaller craft. It's possible they don't have anything in the shape of aircraft flying around Voran. If that's the case, no one will spot us on the roof."

She motioned to Algar. "There's something I want you to do. It won't be easy and almost certainly it will be dangerous."

"If it means I can free my people, I will do anything you ask."

The Amazon took the small welder from her belt and gave it to him. "This will burn through the toughest metal. It's quite simple to use. You just press this stud and it will ignite automatically. Somehow, you have to join those others being kept in that building over there." She indicated the large building at the corner of the street.

"How can he possibly do that?" Mexone queried.

"Quite easily." The Amazon gave a grim smile. "He simply walks out of here and allows himself to be picked up by those guards. They're certain to believe he's somehow escaped from the others. They're not aware he came to Voran on board one of their spaceships and as far as they're concerned there's no other way he could have got here unless they brought him from Thoron."

"And then what do I do?" Algar asked.

"My belief is that once inside that building your people are shackled and no guards are left inside once that door is securely locked. You wait until the opportunity arises and then use this instrument to free everyone. I had hoped to discover where the Vorans keep their weapons but that doesn't seem possible. You'll have to use anything you can lay your hands on."

Summing up, she continued, "Wait until nightfall before you try anything. By that time most of the captives should be inside, waiting to go out on the night shift. Once you're free make your way to the landing field and get on board that spacecraft. We'll try to join you there. In the meantime, I hope to put as many of these machines out of commission as possible."

She pointed towards the door at the far end of the foodstore. "Go now while there seems to be no one around."

Tucking the welder out of sight in his belt, Algar pulled open the door and stepped outside. The Amazon watched him walk out into the middle of the street and then made for the rear door through which they had entered several hours earlier. Outside in the small yard she looked up, scanning the wall in the brightening dawn light. There were no projections here but on top of the wall were two spear-like protuberances.

Taking out the nylon cord she made a loop at one end, then cast it expertly upward. The loop dropped neatly over one of the pointed features. Pulling it tight, she commenced to climb, hand over hand, up the side of the wall. Mexone followed closely. Reaching the top, he knelt beside the Amazon as she replaced the cord in her belt.

The two adjoining walls on either side of the low flat roof rose more than thirty feet into the air. Here, however, there were several of the angular abutments that seemed to be a feature of Voran architecture. It was impossible to guess what function they performed but to the Amazon and Mexone they represented a means of ascending to the top.

Even so, their arm and leg muscles were beginning to ache by the time they reached the roof, swinging themselves from one projection to the next, at times hanging by one hand as they struggled to find secure footholds. Pulling herself onto the roof, the Amazon gripped Mexone's hand and drew him up beside her.

As she had guessed, the roof was perfectly flat with no ornamentation of any kind. Pushing herself into a sitting position, she surveyed all of the other buildings around them. Fortunately, none were as high as this one and she gave a sigh of relief as she saw they could not be seen through the windows of any other building in the vicinity.

"From here we should have an excellent view of everything going on down there," she said finally as she got her breath back. "We should be safe as long as no one thinks of looking up."

They crossed the roof to the side of the building fronting the main street. Already there was plenty of activity down below. Crowds of ordinary civilians moved along the wide sidewalks but there were also plenty of armed soldiers.

"It isn't going to be easy to destroy any of these machines, Vi," Mexone remarked after a while.

Pursing her lips, the Amazon turned her violet eyes towards him. "I realize that. But I don't intend to remain up here and do nothing while Algar is risking his life. We must do something." She pointed to the other side of the roof. "Let's see what's there."

Being completely out of sight of anyone down below, they sprinted for the ledge thirty feet away. Glancing down, they saw there was no gap between them and the adjoining building but the flat roof was some twenty feet lower than the one on which they were standing. Just a short distance from them, however, a thick cable emerged from the wall.

It went down at a steep angle until it disappeared through a wide, circular hole in the top of the adjacent building.

"There's our way down," the Amazon said. The cable was about five inches in diameter and looked capable of bearing their weight. Lying flat with her head and shoulders over the edge, she grabbed the cable, interlinking her fingers over the top. Then, sucking in a deep breath, she swung both legs sideways, thrusting herself away from the wall. Instantly, she dropped into space, tightening the muscles of her arms and shoulders to take her weight.

Hand over hand, she commenced to lower herself down. The cable began to shake and sag ominously as Mexone followed but it held until they reached the bottom and were crouched near the large opening into which the cable disappeared.

"This must be some kind of power line," Mexone said. He now had to raise his voice almost to a shout to be heard above the clamor that came from directly beneath them. He eyed it speculatively. "Perhaps if we were to cut it, that would stop all production down there and—"

The Amazon shook her head. "Far too risky, Mexone," she said, placing her lips close to his ear. "Besides, I mean to destroy this entire building and a few more if I can."

"I don't know how you intend to do that. Even if you succeed, you realize you'll almost certainly kill any of those natives working these machines."

The Amazon hesitated. In her burning desire to destroy as much of the Voran arsenal, she had overlooked the presence of the Thoron slaves. She turned back to the gaping aperture in the roof. "Then at least we can satisfy ourselves just what these creatures are doing."

Gripping the sides of the opening, she eased herself through. A moment later, she vanished. How far she had dropped Mexone couldn't guess. Ten feet or a hundred feet it was impossible to tell.

Then her voice reached him, the words almost drowned out by the throbbing tremors that hammered through the air. "I'm all right. It's only a few feet."

Swinging his legs over the opening, he thrust himself forward; then dropped. His legs hit something solid and he staggered for a moment, struggling to maintain his balance in the dimness as the Amazon thrust out a hand to steady him.

They were in a long narrow space. Strange odors stung their nostrils. At the far end of the long chamber they came upon a flight of narrow stairs evidently leading into the lower rooms. Here the racketing noise was deafening.

Cautiously, taking care where she placed her feet in the darkness, the Amazon moved down the steps with Mexone at her back. A light appeared below them—a nauseous greenish radiance. Then the stairs turned sharply to their left.

Pausing, the Amazon bent forward and peered around the corner. An amazing scene met her gaze. The room some thirty feet below was a hive of frenzied activity. Huge machines stood against the far wall with wide conveyor belts crossing the floor. Lights of all colors flashed on control panels. Oval metal objects emerged from the machines onto the conveyor belts that carried them towards a line of native workers at the end of the room directly below the two watchers.

The Amazon recognized the objects instantly, having seen them once before. The sight of them set alarm bells ringing in her mind. In a low whisper, she murmured:

"They're manufacturing neutron bombs, Mexone. My God, with these they could annihilate an entire planet."

"Neutron bombs?" Mexone looked perplexed.

"That's right. They must have discovered some method of applying tremendous pressure to ordinary atoms. Then the atoms are crushed and the electrons around the nucleus are forced into it, combining with the protons to form neutrons. It happens naturally when certain stars collapse."

Peering over her shoulder, Mexone gave a quick nod. "And this is probably going on all over Voran," he whispered back.

"I'd say that's extremely likely." Her face set in grave lines, the Amazon made to say something more but at that moment a bell rang. The moving conveyors stopped.

Down below, a small group of Voran guards appeared in the open doorway. Brandishing their weapons, they moved among the silent workers, herding them out into the street.

"What's happening?" Mexone questioned softly.

"It seems they're changing shifts." A new look came into her violet eyes. "Now if this place remains empty for just a few minutes, I might be able to do something."

"What can you possibly do, Amazon? You're not going to blow this place up with us still inside."

The Amazon's full lips twitched into a mirthless smile. "Not exactly. But I've seen a bomb like those before. With luck, I may be able to prime one of them to explode say twelve hours from now. By that time, I hope to be off this planet with as many of these natives as possible."

In the huge machine room the last of the natives were being taken out. Once they and the guards had gone the Amazon waited no longer. With swift strides she ran down the stairs towards the rows of bomb stacked carefully against the wall. Expertly, she examined the priming mechanism. Fortunately, it seemed reasonably simple to her. Deftly, she removed the locking key and examined the timing device. The measurement markings meant nothing to her, but she assumed they were marked in fractions of Voran days. Thoughtfully she adjusted the timing device.

Once that was done, she replaced the key, turned, and ran lightly back up the stairs. Less than two minutes later, more guards appeared with a further group of Thorons.

To Mexone, the Amazon said tautly, "I set the priming device on that bomb for what I estimate will be twelve hours from now. That should give us sufficient time for Algar to carry out his part of the plan and get away from here before everything goes up."

"You know that if Algar succeeds in freeing those others, it will stir up a hornet's nest."

"So be it," the Amazon replied with a note of determined resolution in her voice. "This is what we came here for—and this is what we'll do. Now let's get out of here before we're discovered."

Together they climbed back up the stairs. At the top the Amazon came to an abrupt halt, so unexpectedly that Mexone bumped into her. Quickly she pressed a stud on the language translator in her belt. After an incomprehensible reptilian sibilance, the translation came immediately:

"There are the intruders! Cover them!"

The Voran who had spoken glanced in surprise at the Amazon's belt as he heard the English translation. He spoke again, in a harsh, cruel voice.

"So—a language translator device?" He fingered a small black box all of the Vorans wore strapped onto their uniforms, just below the neck. The Amazon guessed they were language converters used for communicating with the slaves they brought from other planets.

"Obviously, from your appearance you are of an unknown alien race. Do not try to reach your weapons. We are quite prepared to kill you now if you make such a move."

Another voice said, "Both of you step forward and keep your hands in sight."

Two Vorans stood a few feet away. Both held blasters in their scaly hands pointed at the two Crusaders.

As he stepped forward Mexone made as if to go for the protonic blaster in his belt.

"Don't be a fool, Mexone!" The Amazon snapped. "They could kill us both before we could harm them."

"You are quite correct," grated the nearer Voran as the Amazon's device transcribed her words to him. "Now remove those blasters from your belts and drop them onto the floor."

Reluctantly, her mind racing, the Amazon pulled the weapon from its holster and let it fall with a thud at her feet. A moment later, Mexone did likewise.

"How you got here is something we do not know," continued the first guard. "However, we shall soon find out. You are both clearly from another planet, come here as spies and saboteurs. Before we kill you, however, you will be questioned. Perhaps there are more of you in the city. If so, I assure you we will soon find them."

"May I ask how you found us?" the Amazon asked, forcing evenness into her voice.

The Voran's wide mouth parted in what was supposed to be a satisfied smile, exposing the pointed teeth. "Since we do not intend to allow you to live much longer, there is no harm in telling you. Evidently you think we are fools and possess no security systems on Voran. There are small cameras in the sky over every city on this world. We use them in the rare event that any of our prisoners should escape and attempt to hide."

"Very clever," Mexone interrupted. "It would seem we've underestimated you."

"And that was your big mistake," snarled the second guard. "The camera picked you up when you climbed onto the roof of the building next to this and relayed the image to our security headquarters where we now intend to take you for interrogation."

Waving his weapon menacingly, the first guard indicated that they were to go back to the roof. There was nothing the Crusaders could do with two weapons leveled at them. At the far end of the room, they pulled themselves through the gap around the thick cable onto the flat roof.

Now they saw there was a strange looking craft parked in the center, obviously a flying machine of some kind. A third Voran sat behind the controls. Once they were seated, the guards climbed on board and the machine lifted into the air.

Knowing that the guards could pick up anything they said, the Amazon kept her thoughts to herself as the flier cruised over the sprawling city. It seemed they had now got a lot more than they had bargained for. She tried desperately to think of a way out of this critical predicament. Now they had fallen into the hands of the Vorans they could expect no leniency or mercy.

She had seen what had happened to that unfortunate native the previous evening when he had attempted to escape. Killing was in the Vorans' nature. Apart from that they appeared to be completely emotionless. Recalling how that Thoron had been killed, she suddenly experienced a faint sense of hope.

These two guards had made no mention of Algar when they had boasted about their surveillance system. Had he been seen leaving a couple of hours earlier, she was sure they would have told of it. But whether Algar had had better luck than they had was problematical.

The flight across the city lasted only a few minutes. Operating the controls, the Voran pilot brought the craft down on the edge of a large square in front of a tall building. In spite of its ugly appearance, this one seemed more imposing than the rest and the Amazon guessed it was the headquarters of the security guards.

Opening the door of the craft, one of the guards stepped out still covering them with his gun as they alighted. When the second guard stepped out he carried two lengths of stout chain. A moment later, the Amazon's arms were pinned against her back and the chain was wrapped tightly around her wrists before being locked.

As Mexone was handcuffed in a similar manner, the Amazon tensed the muscles in her arms and shoulders, testing the strength of the chain. After a few moments she had convinced herself that with her superhuman strength she could break these chains quite easily any time she wished. She flashed Mexone a significant look, and he nodded imperceptibly.

With one guard on each side of them they were marched up the flight of steps and along a short corridor, stopping in front of a large door with Voran symbols on it. One of the guards knocked and then opened the door, thrusting them inside. A tall Voran was seated behind the desk near the window. The insignia on his uniform indicated that he was of a higher rank than the two guards.

The lidless eyes glared at the two prisoners as they were pushed forward with guns in their backs until they stood directly in front of the desk. Glancing down, the Amazon noticed that there was also a language translator in front of him. As he made to switch it on, one of their captors made a negative gesture. "The language of these aliens is unknown to us, sir. But they have their own communication device."

The official looked surprised for a moment, then: "Where did you find them?" the Voran asked.

"They were inside one of the bomb manufacturing units," the guard who had spoken answered deferentially.

The reptilian face assumed a menacing expression as he looked at the captives. "Clearly you come from some other world, sent to spy on us. Where is your spaceship?"

"We have no spaceship," the Amazon replied, meeting the other's direct stare.

A flicker of surprise crossed the Voran's face. Then he said harshly, "No spaceship? Then how did you get here? Do not try to lie to me. We have ways of sifting the truth from falsehoods. Depending on how you answer my questions will decide whether you die quickly— or painfully slowly."

Stoutly, Mexone said, "If we're going to die anyway, why should we answer any of your questions?"

At a gesture from the leader, the guard standing behind Mexone swung a scaly fist, hitting him hard on the side of the head. The blow scarcely hurt but Mexone feigned pain as he jerked his head to one side, going along with the Amazon's strategy of not letting these creatures know how strong they really were.

"So you wish to be stubborn. Very well. Perhaps a few hours in a cell will give you time in which to decide to cooperate."

With a negligent wave of his hand, the Voran turned back to the papers on his desk. The Crusaders were led from the room and taken along a maze of corridors and finally down a long passage which obviously led into the deeper regions of the building. Here there were several doors all with massive metal locks.

One of the guards opened a door and, with a wave of his weapon, signaled that they were to go inside. The Amazon shrugged. At the moment there was nothing they could do but obey. Bending his head beneath the low lintel, Mexone followed her. Behind them the door closed with a loud metallic sound that was followed by the unmistakable click of a key turning in the lock.

CHAPTER 10

DEATH OF A PLANET

STARING around him, Mexone asked tightly, "Is there anything we can do to get out of here, Amazon?"

There was a low bed against one wall but apart from this, the cell was empty. The Amazon shook her blonde head. "Not at the moment, I'm afraid. Things could be a lot worse. I'm wondering why they haven't tried torturing us."

Mexone shrugged. "Perhaps they are. To their alien way of thinking, just being shut up in a confined space may be abhorrent to them."

The Amazon nodded. "That sounds logical. If so, they're going to be disappointed when we fail to crack."

"Look here, Amazon," Mexone said impatiently. "We can break these chains whenever we want, so why—"

"There's no doubt we can break these chains," the Amazon interrupted, "but even if we smashed that door down, we'd be killed before we got outside this building."

Mexone got up and began pacing back and forth. The Amazon watched him, knowing exactly how he felt. Like herself, he was used to action, making snap decisions and acting on them. Inactivity was something that grated on his nerves.

"Sit down, Mexone," she said finally. "There's nothing we can do at the moment but wait."

"That's easy to say. But how much longer do you think they intend to keep us here? Don't forget—that neutron bomb is due to go off as soon as it gets dark. If we're not off the planet by then, we're both dead."

"We've been in tight situations before and come through them. We'll do it again, I promise you." She knew she was only trying to reassure him. At the moment she had no idea how they could extricate themselves from this highly dangerous position.

For almost nine hours they were left languishing in the tiny cell. Then there came the rattle of a key in the door and it was pulled open. Three guards stood there, two with their weapons drawn.

"Evidently they're taking no chances with us," the Amazon muttered as they stepped out into the passage. She activated the translator at her belt.

"No talking," the guard with the key snapped tersely. He thrust the Amazon hard in the back with his gun.

Watched closely by the guards they were taken back into the office. The same official sat behind the desk, his lidless eyes fixed on them. "Perhaps you are now more willing to talk," he said tonelessly.

The Amazon stared coldly at him. In an icy tone, she said, "As I said before, we intend to tell you nothing."

The menacing expression on the Voran's face did not change. He remained silent for a moment as if waiting for her to continue. When she did not, his glance flicked towards the guards. "Take them outside and kill them. Use your molecular disintegrators so there's no trace of them left."

Instantly, the two guards leapt forward and grabbed each of them by the arm, spinning them round so that they faced the door. As they did so, the Amazon gave Mexone a meaningful glance and an almost imperceptible nod. Flexing the steel muscles in her arms, she broke the chains binding her wrists as if they were string as Mexone did the same. Without pausing, she swung her arm in a vicious arc. Instantly, the length of chain wrapped itself around the guard's throat.

With a savage tug, she pulled him off his feet, breaking his neck. By the time she straightened up with the Voran's disintegrator in her hand, Mexone had swung his bunched fist at the other guard's jaw, smashing the bones. Without a sound, the Voran dropped.

Whirling quickly, she leveled the weapon at the official, leaving the third guard to Mexone. Already, the Voran's right hand was moving towards the top drawer of his desk. "Move another inch and you'll be as dead as these three," she said in a deceptively soft voice. "Now walk slowly around the desk. You're going out of here in front of us. If any of your guards try to stop us, I won't hesitate to shoot."

Snarling viciously, the official obeyed. Beside her, Mexone asked, "You think we're going to make it, Amazon?"

Prodding the disintegrator hard into the Voran's back, the Amazon replied, "If we don't, there'll be one less Voran to worry about."

The large doors opened automatically as they approached them and they saw that the day had almost ended. It was twilight outside. They also saw something else. A line of armed Vorans stood at the bottom of the steps leading down into the square. Several carried disintegrators but other held much larger weapons in their hands.

Tightening her finger on the stud of the disintegrator the Amazon said harshly, "Order them to drop their weapons—or I'll kill you now."

The official gave a snort of derision. "You are a fool if you believe that will stop them. For the Voran cause, all of us are dispensable." He raised his head slightly. "I command you to kill these invaders who came to spy our world."

"I think he means it," Mexone said tightly.

"I'm sure he does," the Amazon replied. "It's the ant complex— millions of individuals but only one single mind. But we'll take a lot of them with us." Lashing out with her foot, she kicked the official down the steps, throwing herself to one side and bringing up the disintegrator. A thin beam of light flashed over her head and a large chunk of the building behind her disappeared, leaving a gaping hole.

Rolling onto her left arm, she brought up her own weapon. Aiming swiftly, she pressed the stud, swinging the weapon in a short arc. Four of the Vorans disappeared in blinding flashes of light. Three more were disintegrated by Mexone's expert marksmanship.

In spite of this, the Amazon realized that the Vorans had only to disrupt the molecular structure along the base of the building to bring the entire front of the structure down on their heads.

A sudden sound came from somewhere in the near distance. Her initial thought was that the enemy was bringing up heavier weapons. Then she swung her attention to the wide street at the far corner of the square. It was no longer empty as it had been only a few minutes before. She saw the faint light from the overhead lamps shine on hundreds of tall, blue-skinned figures and leading them was Algar's familiar figure.

Streaming across the square in a silent horde, they fell upon the Vorans from the rear. Lengths of heavy chain smashed scaly flesh and bone to pulp. Taken completely by surprise, the Vorans had no chance to fight back and were being overwhelmed. Moments later, it was all over.

Algar hurried towards them. "We must hurry now. More guards will soon come."

The Amazon patted the native on the arm. "Thanks, Algar. You arrived just in the nick of time. Now we must reach that spaceship and blast off from this planet."

Turning, Algar called something in his strange clicking language. Leaving the dead Vorans, the natives swung round and began running swiftly towards the street. Before following them, the Amazon picked up one of the large, heavy weapons, cradling it in one arm as she raced after the others.

Evidently Algar had informed all of his fellows of the plan for they all raced towards the distant landing field. They were only halfway along the street leading to it when the first Voran guards appeared. Several of the natives tackled them, ignoring the deadly weapons. Some died in disintegrator blasts but the remaineder swarmed over the Vorans, overpowering them by sheer weight of numbers.

Racing ahead of the Thorons, the Amazon reached the metal perimeter fence. She aimed the disintegrator at it, pressing the stud. The beam instantly obliterated a wide section allowing the natives to pour onto the ground beyond.

While Mexone took command of them, urging them to swarm up the ladder into the airlock of the spaceship, the Amazon turned her attention to the other two vessels standing close by. She had no idea what the heavy weapon in her hands would do but aiming at the nearer vessel, she pressed down the small lever at the side.

There was a sharp explosion and the recoil struck viciously along her arm. In the darkness the small projectile was almost invisible as it sped towards its target. It struck the vessel midway up the angular hull. There was a brilliant splash of light where it hit and then a tracery of blue lines spread outward, covering the entire spaceship. The vessel imploded with a thunderous roar.

Finding Mexone at her side, she said, "Obviously the Vorans have weapons we've never even thought of." Without waiting for a reply, she fired a second missile at the other Voran spaceship. The result was exactly the same.

"We're nearly ready to go." Mexone indicated where the last of the natives were climbing swiftly towards the airlock of the remaining craft.

"Then let's go," the Amazon said briskly, "before any of those guards yonder bring up one of these weapons and use it on us."

A minute later everyone was on board and Mexone slammed the airlock door shut as the Amazon ran along the wide corridor towards the control room. Algar led his fellows into the enormous storage hold used for the slaving operation.

"Get everyone to lie flat," she called to him over her shoulder. "I'm going to get maximum power from the engines."

Grateful now that she had spent some time studying the Voran controls, she pressed down a small switch. With a roar, the engines burst into thunderous life, thrusting the huge spaceship into the sky. Below them a barrage of disintegrator beams lanced after them but all fell short as the craft speared through the atmosphere heading for outer space.

The Amazon soon found that the controls were not too different from those on the Ultra, although the arrangement of the various buttons and dials was unfamiliar and the symbols beside them meant absolutely nothing to her. After a few moments she found the button that controlled the visiscreen and they were able to view their surroundings.

The large red sun blazed on their starboard bow, dwindling slowly as they sped away from the Voran system. From the pattern of stars visible on the screen, she judged that the enemy sun was situated some twenty light years inside the rim of the Andromeda Nebula. The star system in which Uxxar had appeared was located on the very rim of the Nebula and the Amazon knew from the relatively short time they had been in hyperspace on the journey from Uxxar to the Voran home planet, it could not be too far away.

"We still have a couple of problems to face, Amazon, even though we have succeeded in escaping from Voran." Mexone stood beside her, his restless gaze wandering over the multitude of stars visible on the visiplate.

"And what are they, Mexone?" the Amazon asked quietly.

"Firstly, how do you hope to locate Uxxar from among all of these stars out there? It would be difficult enough in our own galaxy but this is the Andromeda Nebula and completely unknown to us. Secondly, if we do reach Uxxar and return to the other end of that wormhole, Abna is sure to be watching for us. If he spots a Voran spaceship leaving Uxxar his first reaction will be to attack it."

The Amazon sat in pensive thought for several moments before replying. Then she said, "The first problem should not be too difficult. I'm going to scan all of the double star systems within twenty light years. I kept track of the time we were in hyperspace, and we couldn't have traveled much further than that. I'll grant you there may be several but not with the special characteristics we are looking for."

"Which are?" Mexone was still not convinced of her reasoning.

"A blue giant sun and a seetee yellow companion with only three planets, one of which—Uxxar—will soon be passing between the two solar components."

"And the second problem?" Mexone persisted.

"We'll face that one when we come to it. Now help me to locate Uxxar."

Working together as a team the Amazon and Mexone quickly scanned all of the double star systems, rejecting almost all of them for one reason or another until only two possible candidates remained. Both were situated close to the rim of the Andromeda Galaxy.

The Amazon glanced at her wrist chronometer. "We don't have time to visit them both," she remarked. Leaning over the controls, she turned the small dial next to the visiplate button. As she had hoped, it magnified the images on the screen.

"Now we are getting somewhere," she murmured. Deftly, she manipulated the unfamiliar controls bringing first one of the double star systems into view and then the other. "That's the one," she exclaimed confidently. "The other system has at least six planets."

Pushing the magnification to its limit, they easily picked out the Jupiter-like outer world and Thoron. A moment later, they spotted Uxxar.

The Amazon tightened her lips as she aligned the ship towards the Thoron system. "All we can do now it pray that the Voran spaceships use the same method of entering hyperspace as the Ultra— by automatically entering hyperspace as the ship nears the speed of light."

Without any hesitation, she thrust the drive lever forward as far as it would go. As their velocity increased the stars on the viewing screen became noticeably bluer. For several minutes the shriek of the engines screamed in their ears. Both of the Crusaders struggled to remain conscious as the acceleration crushed them.

Then, abruptly, came the feeling of nausea as they were twisted into another dimension. The visiscreen showed only an enigmatic swirling gray mist. The high-pitched screech ceased. They were in hyperspace.

* * * *

Now everything depended upon the vessel's automatic controls. The Amazon was gambling that the journey to Uxxar was pre-programmed. If they came out into normal space too soon there would still be several light years to cross before they reached their destination. If they remained too long in hyperspace they would overshoot Uxxar.

Hours passed. Mexone watched the Amazon anxiously as she performed swift mental computations in her mind, glancing at her chronometer.

"Time's nearly up," she announced. "Just about the same duration in hyperspace as on the outward journey—"

Again that brief, anguishing inside-out feeling. Normally the Crusaders were unconscious at this point on a hyperspace voyage, but they had not dared to sleep on this journey.

Mexone did he realize he had been holding his breath until it burned in his lungs. In front of them the viewing screen came back to life.

Uxxar was visible as a large disc barely a million miles away!

"You did it!" Mexone was unable to keep the relief from his voice.

The Amazon did not answer. Her slim yellow fingers moved smoothly over the controls, reducing their tremendous velocity as she turned the spaceship towards the planet. At the moment their forward speed was far too high to attempt a landing and she was not certain how much deceleration this vessel could take without breaking up.

The surface of the planet came closer at an alarming rate. She had already made up her mind to land in the arid desert rather than on that island in the middle of the large ocean. They entered the atmosphere an hour later. After making a single orbit, she judged their speed was sufficiently low to land.

Without taking her attention from the controls, she said, "Hang on. We are going down now."

Approaching the surface at a small angle, she lowered the huge vessel until it hit the surface, sliding over the soft sand for two miles before it came to a stop. For a moment she remained absolutely still, then turned to face Mexone standing three feet away.

"Well, we made it. Better check on Algar and his fellows to see if they're all right."

"They will be," Mexone asserted confidently. "Don't forget this ship's hold has been especially designed for transporting slaves through hyperspace. Probably the floor of the hold is covered by acceleration cushioning materials."

The Amazon smiled. "Of course. Then all we have to do is wait for Uxxar to reach its transition orbit—and that will be fairly soon…"

* * * *

The Ultra hung motionless in space some fifty million miles above the spot where the orbit of Uxxar passed between the blue giant and yellow seetee suns. Standing in front of the control panel, Abna's gaze probed the blackness where Uxxar should reappear at any moment.

"What should we do if they don't come back?" There was an expression of deep concern on Viona's face.

Abna tried to reassure her. "You know your mother, Viona. If there is only one in a million chance of them getting back, she will find it."

"I hope so." Viona moved away and sank into one of the seats. After a little while, she glanced up. "You still have not answered my question."

Abna shrugged. "In the unlikely event of that happening, then we'll land on Uxxar and take the Ultra to wherever that wormhole leads us. If the others are in some kind of trouble, it will be up to us to get them out of it."

"Certainly that would be better than just sitting around here." Thania came over to look at the scene outside. "There is also something else we have to take into consideration. Even if the Amazon and Mexone have succeeded in landing back on Uxxar, the Vorans will also certainly send more of their spaceships back to collect another batch of the natives from Thoron."

"Then we must be ready for them," Abna replied grimly. "Now the hull has been repaired on Thoron, we can give a good account of ourselves." He turned at a slight sound behind him.

Dorem came into the control room. Shortly before they had blasted off from Thoron, he had asked Abna's permission to go with them on this mission to watch for Uxxar's expected return. He had said nothing of his reasons for wanting to accompany them but Abna guessed he was anxious to know whether Algar was still alive and what had happened to those friends of his who had been taken away as prisoners of the Vorans.

Standing at Abna's shoulder, he made to say something; then pointed urgently at the screen. For a few moments he gabbled something in his own language; then switched to English. "There is Uxxar! Do you see it?"

"He's right!" Thania cried. "Down there between the two suns. I can see it clearly."

Abna gave a quick nod. Swiftly, he increased the magnification until the surface features of the planet were clearly visible. Even as they watched, something moved and a moment later they all saw the ugly shape of a Voran spacecraft lifting from the surface facing the blue sun.

"A Voran ship," Viona said despondently. "And judging by its trajectory it's coming straight for us," she added. "I'll put the weapon systems on alert." She hurried to the far side of the control room.

Abna studied the swiftly approaching enemy spaceship closely. There was something nagging at the back of his mind, something important—but he could not think what it was. Then he knew what was bothering him. That vessel had taken off from the arid hemisphere, not from the ocean where the Voran camp was situated.

"Hold your fire, Viona!" he shouted urgently. On the screen, the Voran spaceship suddenly began to tilt from one side to the other as if the pilot was trying to attract his attention. "Those are not Vorans on that spaceship. It's your mother piloting it."

Ten minutes later, the Voran craft had drawn alongside the Ultra and they could clearly see the Amazon at the controls. She made a downward motion with her hand, pointing in the direction of Thoron. Abna raised his right hand to acknowledge that he understood.

The journey down to Thoron was soon completed. Side by side, the Ultra and the Voran spaceship landed in the wide clearing where the small pinnace still stood. Throwing open the Ultra's airlock, Abna clambered down the ladder with Viona, Thania and Dorem close behind him. They stood waiting impatiently until the Voran airlock popped open.

The Amazon was the first out with Mexone behind her. Going forward, Abna put his arms around the Amazon and kissed her. For a moment, she looked surprised and then gave a brief smile as Viona rushed past them and embraced Mexone.

Above them, the first of the natives were beginning to descend the ladder, staring about them as if unable to believe they were home.

"We managed to save more than two hundred of them," the Amazon said after first Thania and then Viona had released her from a hug. "Unfortunately we couldn't rescue more."

"At least these are safe," Algar stepped forward. "And for that we thank you. I am sure our chief will be—how do you say—honored if you would remain with us for a few days."

"I wish that was possible, Algar," the Amazon said, smiling. "Unfortunately, we still have one more task to perform and then we must be on our way. There are many other worlds where people like you are at the mercy of arrogant, warlike races."

Algar looked disappointed but finally he nodded. "As you wish," he said gravely. "We will never forget the Cosmic Crusaders who came from the sky to help us."

"Yet we still fear the return of the Vorans," Dorem put in. "Once you are gone there is nothing to stop them taking us back to their world."

"You need have no fear of them ever coming back," the Amazon told him. "Before we leave your solar system I intend to make sure they can never return. You have my word on that."

Once Algar and Dorem had followed the others into the jungle, the Amazon and Abna brought each other up to date on their experiences.

"But Vi," Abna finished, "what did you mean when you told Algar you'll make sure the Vorans don't come back here? Your gambit with that neutron bomb may hold them up for a while, but they'll soon regroup their forces."

"You'll see," the Amazon replied mysteriously. "I want the four of you to transport twenty of the most powerful nuclear bombs from the Ultra into the control cabin of the Voran spaceship and prime them to explode on impact. In the meantime I will make some adjustments to the controls of the vessel so that I can operate them from on board the Ultra."

Viona wrinkled her brow in bewilderment. "What will that achieve?" she asked bluntly.

"Quite a lot if everything goes well. The only way we can stop the Vorans from invading this, or any other system in this region of space, is to utterly destroy Uxxar. I mean to fly both spaceships close to Uxxar and then crash the Voran ship on the hemisphere facing away from the seetee sun. I'm hoping that such a colossal nuclear explosion will be sufficient to alter its orbit so that it spirals into that sun, thereby destroying this end of that ultra-dimensional wormhole."

"Wouldn't it be simpler if we were to use the Zero Thought Amplifier?" Thania suggested.

"It might," the Amazon agreed. "But somehow I think it would be more poetic if we used one of their own creations to deny them any further access to our galaxy."

* * * *

Standing in front of the huge viewing screen, the five Cosmic Crusaders watched as the Voran spacecraft sped downward towards Uxxar. Abna had used his mathematical skills to pinpoint the exact point of impact, which would give the maximum effect. Now, traveling at half light speed, the alien vessel could just be seen against the brilliant surface.

Ten seconds later, it speared through the atmosphere, glowing brightly. Then the glare of the nuclear detonation obliterated more than a hundred square miles of the desert. A huge mushroom cloud climbed thousands of feet into air.

"Do you think even that explosion will be enough to move a planet?" Viona queried.

"We haven't moved it," Abna told her. "But we *have* slowed it down in its pell-mell orbit around that giant star. That should mean that it will become fatally enmeshed in the star's gravity field."

Abna's theory proved correct. As time passed, Uxxar was drifting ever nearer to the seetee sun. Closer, ever closer, it came as the tremendous gravitational pull of the yellow sun drew the planet towards it. Then the end came with an almost dramatic suddenness.

One second the planet was visible as a round black spot against the glaringly bright solar surface—the next instant there was a dazzling flash as colossal amounts of matter and antimatter annihilated each other.

"Excellent," the Amazon murmured. "That massive explosion will also have completely destroyed that wormhole. Those vessels from the Andromeda Nebula can no longer use it as a shortcut."

"I've just had an uneasy thought," Viona said slowly. "With both the planet and the wormhole removed, so is Uxxar's gravitational influence. What if that should upset Thoron's orbit, so that it starts to spiral inwards?"

"It won't," Abna said decisively. "Since Uxxar is the innermost planet in the system and the other two, unlike Uxxar, revolve around both suns, its destruction will have the effect of moving Thoron into a slightly *larger* orbit since Uxxar's gravitational pull on Thoron will no longer exist. Compared with the gravitational effects of the two suns and the large outermost planet, this would be negligible—but not zero of course."

Abna smiled, then added: "According to my calculations, the amount of energy produced by the total annihilation of Uxxar by matter-antimatter interaction will be sufficient not only to stabilize Thoron in its slightly wider orbit, but to also raise the temperature of the seetee sun enough to compensate for the fact that the planet is a little more distant."

Turning away from the stupendous sight, the Amazon said quietly. "That being so, I think our task here is finished. It's time to leave.

There are millions of other planets out there and so far we have only visited a mere handful of them."

"Haven't you forgotten that barrier the Vorans erected?" Thania inquired. "We can't penetrate that—not even in hyperspace. You told us that the Vorans had adjusted it, remember?"

"Somehow I think we'll find it no longer exists, Thania." The Amazon gave a wry smile. "There was only one place the Vorans could obtain the tremendous energy needed to build that barrier—from that wormhole. Now it's gone the power to maintain it no longer exists."

Which was exactly what they found—as the Ultra sped away from the edge of the galaxy towards the millions of stars that glittered like diamonds across the entire length and breadth of the viewing screen.